COFFEE BOY

AUSTIN CHANT

ALSO BY AUSTIN CHANT

Peter Darling

> *A queer, trans retelling of Peter Pan in which Pan returns to Neverland after growing up in the real world, only to be drawn into a vicious and sensual conflict with his old enemy, Captain Hook.*

Caroline's Heart

> *A queer Western laced with fantasy and romance in which Cecily, a reclusive witch, is torn between using her most powerful magic to resurrect her long-dead lover or to save the life of a stranger.*

Coffee Boy

Austin Chant

Amanda deserves accolades for a lot of things, but especially for making me write this book. (Twice.)

COFFEE BOY

1.

Kieran expected Heidi Norton's campaign office to involve a fancy building. A stern exterior. Heavy security. Something intimidating, or at least austere.

Instead, the San Antonio branch of the Norton campaign resides on the top floor of a completely average commercial building. The elevator is slow, the floor is plasticky, and fluorescent lights flicker out of a speckled gray ceiling. The sign on the office door is crooked, and inside there's a jumble of cramped desks and cramped people mixed in with printers and filing cabinets. The door is ajar and the windows are open, letting in a trickle of summer breeze, but it's still agonizingly hot.

Kieran stands in the door for a long moment,

his work-appropriate satchel clasped under his arm, feeling altogether more anxious than he wanted to. His pronoun pin gleams on the lapel of a shirt he neglected to iron, and his binder's already sticky with sweat. A few people turn to look at him.

Kieran clears his throat. "Hi? I'm the new intern."

A middle-aged white lady sitting at the desk nearest to Kieran gives him a benevolent smile. "That's right! I forgot we were getting someone new. I'm Marie. Finances."

"Kieran." He stretches across her desk to shake Marie's hand, then settles stiffly back against the door. "I don't know about finances, but I'm excited to get started." If he says it often enough, maybe it'll become true. "Nice to meet you."

Marie nods, smiling. "You'll want to talk to Seth, dear. He's in his office right now."

Seth? The name is unfamiliar, and Kieran blanches. "Wait, is Marcus here? I was supposed to see Marcus."

Marie shakes her head. "No, no, he won't be in until later. Seth handles everything when Marcus isn't around."

"Okay." It's *not* okay. Kieran feels his guts freeze. It's bad enough that Marcus got him into this whole internship situation—now he's not even around to handle the introductions? Kieran smothers his nerves and scans the room, catching sight of the one other door. "Is that Seth's office?"

Marie tuts and waves him back. "Now, wait a minute. He said he was making an important phone call. You don't want to interrupt Seth when he's on the phone!" She chuckles, and a few people nearby laugh uncomfortably. "Have a seat, dear. He'll be out soon."

There's really nowhere to sit except at a chair across from Marie's desk, like he's settling in for a consultation. Kieran sits, unwillingly. He's hoping Marie will go back to work and let him fade into the background, but she keeps watching him. He smiles vaguely and averts his eyes.

She leans forward anyway, clearly intent on engaging him. "Kieran, you *are* the administrative intern, aren't you?"

"That's me."

"Oh, that's so funny." Marie beams. "Marcus thought you were a *boy*." She winks, like they're sharing a joke. When Kieran stiffens and stares at her, the smile slowly slides off her face. "I'm sorry. I'm sure it was just a mistake—"

"He wasn't wrong," Kieran snaps.

He waits for some kind of clarity to dawn on Marie, but she just looks more and more confused. He feels himself blushing. "I'm a guy," he says, loudly. "Thanks."

"I'm sorry," Marie repeats, bafflement written all over her face. She's studying him like she just can't make the pieces fit.

Kieran grips his knees. Trust Marcus to promise him a *trans-friendly workplace* and not even bother to find out if anyone around him is trans-friendly.

"It's your hair," Marie says finally, with hopeful satisfaction. "I'm just not used to seeing such long hair on boys—"

"Yeah. I get it." Even to his own ears, his voice sounds sharp and mean. Kieran can feel people turning to look at them, probably as bewildered as Marie, and he suddenly needs to get out of the room. He can't handle the mystified stares or the inevitable questions that come any time he tries to say who he is.

His options are hiding in the hallway outside or diving deeper into hell, and if he walks out of the office now, he's pretty sure he'll never be able to make himself go back in. He squares his shoulders, gets up, and walks brusquely over to Seth's door. He ignores Marie's hurried protest and knocks, hard.

Because honestly, fuck this guy's phone call.

It feels like approximately forever before the door finally opens. A tall, thin guy with black hair—Seth, presumably—glares down at Kieran from the doorway. He has a landline phone pressed to his ear, the cord stretching away toward a desk across the room.

Kieran can hear somebody mumbling through the phone. Seth presses a hand over the mouthpiece and hisses, "*What?*"

Kieran feels an internal shriveling when Seth looks at him, like he's being dissected. Seth has bright, cutting eyes and an unshakable stare and a cold, angular face. He lands right at the intersection of *scary* and *scary hot*, and for a second Kieran doesn't know what to do with the mixture of hostility and intrigue twisting in his gut.

If he were a lesser man, he'd probably clutch his satchel to his chest to put a barrier between them. But Kieran is not a lesser man, and he *really* wants out of this room, so he slings his satchel over his shoulder and adopts a presumptuous smile. "Good morning," he says. "Kieran Mullur. New intern." He looks past Seth to see three desks and a couple of table fans working overtime. Perfect. "Mind if I put my stuff down in here?"

The look on Seth's face says that he does mind—his eyebrow twitches a little—but he jerks his head angrily toward the middle desk and retreats from the door.

Kieran scoots inside and shuts the door with a shudder of relief. Okay. This is not his best first impression ever, but no one's ever pegged him for the friendly type.

At least this office is quieter, bigger, and better aerated than the other room. One desk—Kieran's, presumably—is barren; Seth's is painfully neat, with stacks of paperwork separated by colored tabs, matching sets of pens and highlighters arranged in precise rows, everything squared and symmetrical. The third desk has stickers stuck all down one side and a shiny desktop computer somewhat marred by a peeling "Hello, my name is MARCUS" label on the back of the monitor. Typical Marcus.

When his heart has stopped pounding, Kieran crosses the room and sinks gratefully into the chair at his new desk.

Although it might not be his desk for long if Seth kills him. Luckily, Seth looks like he's too busy tearing somebody to shreds over the phone to spare much malice for Kieran. Every time he stops to listen to whatever the caller is saying, his nose wrinkles contemptuously. He's keeping his voice down, but Kieran catches something about "funding that was promised to us" and "pulling all mention of your business from our campaign materials".

In Kieran's assessment, Seth looks kind of like a grown-up Boy Scout—that straightlaced, proper, honest look—but also kind of like a snake. He's at least thirty, perfectly clean-shaven, sleek. He has hair trimmed short and blunt, long on top but slicked down, and despite the heat, he's wearing a crisp blazer. The only part of his look that seems out of place is a single steel stud in his right ear, and even that is vaguely intimidating.

Awesome.

Feeling intimidated doesn't stop Kieran from wanting to eavesdrop, though, because he wants a distraction as much as he relishes drama. He takes out his phone and pretends to be distracted by Twitter while listening as hard as he can. Seth's side of the conversation is choppy, as if he's being interrupted.

"I can't be any clearer about this," Seth says. "The senator does not offer business endorsements in exchange for donations. If a member of her staff told you otherwise, I—*sincerely*—apologize." He listens intently for a moment and out of the corner of his eye, Kieran watches Seth squeeze the phone like he wishes it were someone's neck. "No, that's—no, there are no exceptions. Absolutely not. I suggest you contact the main office if you have any more concerns, because as I've said, this is a branch office. I can*not* take a message for the senator, because she doesn't work here. Yes. Goodbye."

Seth smacks the phone down in its cradle, and Kieran jumps in spite of himself. He stuffs his cell phone back into his pocket as Seth swivels toward him.

"So," Seth says. He stands up, offering his hand without approaching Kieran's desk. Kieran has to scramble out of his chair and across the room to shake it, while Seth stares imperiously down at him.

Kieran isn't surprised to find Seth's handshake firm and unforgiving. "Hi," Kieran says, forcing a smile. "Sorry for, um, barging in. I was expecting Marcus." It's only half a lie.

Seth raises his eyebrows. "Marcus mentioned that he knew you. From the university?"

"Yeah. He taught a bunch of my classes." Kieran does his best to sound calm, smooth, anything but as shaky as he feels. "So—who're you? The manager?"

"Marcus is the manager," Seth says, like Kieran should have known. This probably falls into the category of 'Things Marcus Could've Bothered to Tell Kieran.' "I'm Seth Harker, the senior campaign strategist."

The way he says *senior* makes it sounds like he has power over Kieran's life and death. Kieran resists the urge to grimace. "Nice to meet you. Is Marcus going to be here?"

"He had a family engagement. Have a seat, and we'll talk through your responsibilities."

"Okay." Kieran scrunches himself into the chair in front of Seth's desk.

Seth sits across from him, studying Kieran with an awkward level of scrutiny. "What is that button?" he asks.

The pronoun pin. Kieran feels a sharp blush rise in his face again. He's not ashamed of needing to wear it—he's annoyed that he has to. "My pronouns," he says, as casually as he can. "I like to wear it when I meet new people."

Seth gives a mere nod. "I see. As a reminder?"

Kieran flips his thick, curly hair angrily over one shoulder. "Well, most people make the wrong assumption when they meet me."

"Marcus has been very specific in calling you 'he' whenever he mentioned the new intern," Seth says, "so hopefully there won't be any room for wrong assumptions."

His voice is crisp and cool, like it isn't an issue for him at all. Kieran lets out a breath, startled and relieved and angry. Because it *is* an issue, but at least he's not going to have to repeat the conversation he had with Marie. "Great. You might wanna clear that up with the rest of the office."

Seth raises an eyebrow. "Why? Did something happen?"

Kieran is *not* going to fall into the trap of complaining about his coworkers on his first day. "No. It's fine. I just—I didn't get the impression that they knew."

"I see."

Seth actually turns and scribbles something down on a pad of paper in front of him. Kieran can't imagine what he's writing. "Remind everyone in the office that new intern is a dude"? Or, probably more likely, "Fire whiny trans guy at earliest opportunity."

Seth turns back to him. "Let me know if you have any problems." He waits for Kieran to nod. Kieran wonders how obvious it is that he doesn't find this reassuring at all. "Now—Marcus said that he knew you before you applied for the internship. He was impressed with your undergraduate coursework."

More like: Marcus is a bleeding-heart PhD candidate who thinks all trans people are brave and inspiring, and he'd been willing to overlook Kieran's often-lackluster college coursework and pretend it was a sign that Kieran wasn't being challenged enough by the material. And that's why Kieran has the internship. "Yeah, he thought I was okay." Kieran shrugs. "Of course, I'm guessing I'll probably do less campaign strategizing and more... getting coffee and making copies?"

Seth almost smiles. It's a flicker at the corner of his thin little mouth. "You aren't wrong. But we need you for more than that. This is a new branch of Senator Norton's campaign, and things are just starting to get off the ground. You'll be assisting Marcus with whatever he needs to keep us organized, and taking on whatever additional duties we might need an extra hand with. Especially social media and the new campaign website—Marcus said you have some skills in that area, and we're lacking staff with... digital experience."

Kieran translates that to *everyone who works here is old*. "Uh, yeah. I can help with that."

Seth nods approvingly. "I think you'll find the experience rewarding. Our internship program offers you a chance to learn the types of skills it takes to run a campaign. Working on our digital outreach puts you at the intersection of a lot of departments. It might help you see what kind of a real job would suit you."

"A real job?" Kieran laughs in spite of himself, because it stings. "I have one of those already."

"Oh?"

"Flipping burgers," Kieran says. "It comes with real paychecks and everything."

Seth frowns. Kieran can see the cogs turning in his head and wonders if he's smart enough to figure out that Kieran's definition of *real* is "pays rent." Evidently Seth does, because he clears his throat and says, "There will be opportunities for advancement here. Paid advancement. *Assuming*, of course, that you fit the position."

Kieran is pretty sure he won't.

* * *

Seth finds a substantial amount of busywork for Kieran to do, which means that Kieran manages to hide in his office until Marcus arrives. That's when things get interesting.

Marcus breezes in wearing a logo T-shirt and the same thick-rimmed, nerdy glasses he always wore when Kieran took his classes in college. Kieran peeks out of the inner office to see Marcus wandering between desks, exchanging personal greetings and chitchat with every person he passes. He smiles easily at everyone in the office, and everyone smiles back, relaxed—except Seth, who actually stands up at his desk when Marcus walks in, like they're in the military. Kieran half expects him to salute.

"Good morning!" Marcus says brightly, though it's half past two. "Kieran! It's so good to see you again. Seth, I can't believe you're wearing a *blazer* in this weather. Take that thing off. You look like you're frying."

Seth looks away with a huff and sinks back into his chair. He starts unrolling his perfectly crisp cuffs. "I've been getting Kieran set up."

"Good, good, good." Marcus flops into his chair. "I know it's the internship cliché, but everyone's roasting out there. I think a round of iced coffees is in order—Kieran, would you mind getting some?"

"Not at all, sir," Kieran drawls. Marcus winks at him.

"I'll give you the company card," Seth says. "I do track the purchases made on this, just so you're aware."

"Seth!" Marcus chides. "When has an intern ever robbed us on the way to Starbucks?"

Seth purses his lips and doesn't look up from his desk while he hands Kieran the card. From what Kieran has gathered so far, Marcus is actually the one in charge—not least because he's the senator's nephew—but Seth is the power behind the throne, and like the jaded uncle in a Disney movie, he covets Marcus's authority.

Which is why the next thing out of Seth's mouth is so weird. "Marcus, do you want your coffee with caramel?"

"Oh, that would be nice."

Seth fixes Kieran with a stern look. "It's the Starbucks down the block," he says, with the attitude of a commanding officer delivering orders to a new recruit. "Take a right when you exit the building. Call the office if you get turned around. Get twelve sixteen-ounce iced coffees, and get one of them with soy milk and two pumps of caramel syrup."

"Okay," Kieran says, unable to stop himself from smirking. "You must've been the intern before me."

"I was not." Seth glances meaningfully at the door, and Kieran gets on his way. He probably shouldn't antagonize his superiors *too* much on day one.

But who's he kidding? What else would he do?

* * *

Jillian texts him while he's buying coffee, with her usual optimism: *how's your first day going?? Love you! Kick ass!*

And then a series of heart emojis.

Kieran tries to think of something positive to respond with, but positive affirmations are sort of his weak point. Finally he just writes *I'll call you later* and doesn't realize how foreboding that sounds until he's already sent it. He follows up with a couple smiley faces in the hopes of softening the blow.

He's briefly the most popular boy in the office when he comes back with iced coffee and circles around the desks, dropping off frosty plastic cups for everyone. It's a good way to let them see his pronoun pin, too, and to firmly introduce himself by name. A couple people still look confused but don't say anything.

With the last three coffees in hand—including the very special one with soy milk and caramel—Kieran wanders back into Marcus's office.

Marcus is standing behind Seth's desk, leaning

over to study something on his laptop. "I think it's a good start," he's saying, with his usual broad smile. "I like the new angle." Speaking of angles, Seth is angled all away from Marcus, reclining in his chair in a pose so carefully arranged that it looks, from the doorway, incredibly uncomfortable. Like he can't stand to touch Marcus at all. He's running his fingers around the collar of his shirt as if proximity to Marcus makes him sweat.

While Kieran watches, unobserved, Seth rearranges his perfect hair until it's oddly unkempt—and then averts his eyes when Marcus glances at him.

Unfortunately, when he looks away, Seth notices Kieran standing there with three coffees and an inquisitive eyebrow raised, and his expression becomes steely. "Were you planning on distributing those coffees?"

"Of course," Kieran says. "I just didn't want to interrupt whatever you were looking at. But, uh, it sure looks like you could use a cold drink."

Seth's face colors. "It's hot in here," he says defensively.

"Yeah, that's what I meant."

"We were just looking at the new lawn flyers,"

Marcus says cheerfully, straightening up. "Is that my coffee? That was speedy! I think you beat our last intern by at least a minute."

Kieran offers him the caramel coffee and Marcus beams. "Now get settled back in and I'll walk you through the systems we use for organizing our mailing list—it'll probably be second nature for a young guy like you!"

Seth has flipped open a hand mirror and is smoothing his hair back into place. He doesn't look up when Kieran places his coffee on the desk; he barely mumbles a "thank you."

Kieran shakes his head and gets ready for a riveting lesson in campaign administration.

2.

Jillian calls him up that night as he's boiling water for ramen. "Hey, you!" she says. "Guess who's a little jerk and sent me *one* super-mysterious text all day?"

Kieran rolls his eyes at the ceiling, smiling. "I was at the internship. Working."

"Yes, and I was worried about you. So how was it? Was I right and it was totally fine?"

Kieran pauses, because he hates disappointing Jillian. She's the one who bullies him into doing all the things he should do but doesn't want to—like this internship, for example—and she's his first line of defense against total apathy. It was mostly for her sake that he finally agreed to take the internship, and resigned himself to sticking it out at least long enough that she won't be crushed when he gives up. "Yeah, it was okay."

"O*kay?*" Jillian says. "I need the full story." With her usual optimism, she ignores his silence. "How's Marcus? Still handsome?"

"Ugh, Jill, he's never been handsome."

"You have no taste! I had such a crush on him when I was going through my hot-professor phase." She waits for him to reply, but Kieran is short a witty answer. He's exhausted. "All right," Jillian says. "I'm coming over and you can tell me *all* about it."

"You don't have to," Kieran says, although he already knows—before he even says it—that Jillian's only answer will be to scoff into the phone and hang up. He adds more water to the pan and tosses in a second brick of ramen. Jillian gets hungry when she plays counselor.

They met in college. Kieran was the lonely, angry back-row queer who glared at his professors but never called them out on anything; Jillian was the gorgeous butch who would chew her professors out for failing to mention LGBT people in their human rights curriculum, who walked around wearing a Bi Pride pin on her bag every day for four years and sneered at anyone who gave her shit for it. And, for the brief but intense period where Kieran was panicking over the revelation that he was gay *and* trans—like, how doomed to failure could he possibly be?—Jillian was his rock.

Well, *is* his rock. Which she proves by stomping up to his door with an enormous jug of sweet tea under her arm, and cooing sympathetically while Kieran complains about his day. "Oh, babe," she says, when he's finished. "I hope it gets better."

"Me too," Kieran says. Mostly for her benefit, because he's a pessimist. "Crazy thing, though. I'm pretty sure Mister *Senior* Campaign Strategist has a thing for Marcus."

"Nice," Jillian says. "See, I'm not the only one!"

Kieran pokes the side of her ramen bowl with his toe—not enough to make it slosh, just enough to make her shriek and slap his foot away. "Is that not *weird* to you?"

"Why? Are you saying mean, bitter people can't be queer?" Jillian pats his foot. "Look in the mirror."

Kieran grumbles, draping his arms over his face. "I just don't get it. If he's queer, that's... fine." Kieran feels kind of funny about it. He really hadn't expected any of his coworkers to be like him, let alone someone in charge. *Let alone someone attractive.* He can't stop thinking about that one little earring Seth was wearing, so out of place with the rest of his grown-up office worker ensemble. He imagines Seth and Marcus kissing and grimaces. "Like, whatever, Seth can do his thing. But why *Marcus*?"

Jillian mimics his incredulous tone: "'Oh my God, sometimes people have different preferences than me!' Babe, if you don't like the guy anyway, why are you so surprised that he likes someone you don't?"

Kieran grumbles and doesn't say anything, because he's honestly not sure. Maybe it's because, even though Seth is frigid and scary, Kieran had been kind of into the angry tone he'd used on the phone. Kieran can imagine himself tearing someone to shreds over campaign donations in that no-nonsense, condescending tone, but he can't imagine having the guts to do it in real life (and get paid for it). So he'd been prepared to respect Seth, or to just enjoy listening to his phone calls, but knowing that he likes Marcus puts a damper on Kieran's opinion of him.

At least, worst-case scenario, it's funny to watch.

Jillian gets bored of watching him wrestle with his thoughts and nudges him in the shoulder. "Hey, on the topic of Seth—if he's ready to go to bat for you with your coworkers, that's cool! You should tell him what happened with Marie. He'd probably crack down."

Kieran loves Jillian, but sometimes he wonders which version of the world she lives in. "Yeah, no, I'd rather not start this train wreck off by ratting out my coworkers. Also, no offense, but I don't trust a cis guy to know his shit when it comes to *educating the office staff*."

She doesn't say anything, which probably means he's being a bitter pill and she's run out of reassuring words for the night. Kieran sighs into his arms. "Sorry. Wanna watch stupid movies?"

"Sure," Jillian says. She squeezes his foot. "Promise me you're not gonna quit tomorrow."

"I promise," Kieran mutters. It's how she used to get him through class when he threatened to drop out. Just one day after the next, till the end of the semester.

He wonders when he'll get to the end of this job.

* * *

In the first month of his internship, Kieran learns five important things:

A. People who work on political campaigns have ridiculous Starbucks orders and yeah, being the intern means learning them all and balancing twelve cups of coffee on his way back up to the office.

B. Kieran's duties as "administrative intern" aren't extremely specific. They're more general, like, "Do everything that Marcus sucks at."

C. Marcus would honestly be better off as a kindergarten teacher or a knitting instructor than as a campaign manager. Scratch that—he doesn't have the organizational skills to do either of those jobs. He's the most scattered person Kieran has ever met, and he doesn't like bossing his subordinates around. So Kieran is there to organize shit for him, and Seth is there to give orders to the troops. Marcus mostly seems to think his job is raising morale, approving of everyone's work, and making sure they all get enough coffee. He's clearly only employed because he's Heidi Norton's nephew. Although, to be fair, Kieran is only employed because he was Marcus's favorite student.

D. Seth is pretty much a cold fish. Which is a shame, because he's still hot, and he's the only one in the office who's never screwed up Kieran's pronouns. He calls Kieran "he" with military precision, each time with a careful moment's pause before the word.

E. Seth isn't as intimidating as everyone else thinks, because he's crushing hard on their boss.

E is Kieran's favorite point. If he's being entirely honest, half the reason he studied politics in college was because he liked the drama. If it weren't enough that Seth can't seem to deal with being physically close to Marcus without turning red as a tomato, he also gets distracted any time Marcus comes in to work wearing something sleeveless. While Seth stares intensely at anyone else when he's talking to them—like he's daring them to waste a second of his time—when it's Marcus, he gets suddenly quiet and humble and barely makes eye contact.

As disappointed as Kieran is in Seth's taste in men, and as annoyed as he is that the other apparently queer guy in the office is smitten with Kieran's boring ex-professor, it *is* pretty entertaining. Plus, Kieran likes the fact that being queer makes him a good sleuth; he's sure that Seth's painfully obvious crush is invisible to all the wide-eyed cis heterosexuals working at this office, but Kieran is pretty old hat at noticing when people aren't straight.

Unfortunately for Seth, Kieran also notices that there's a picture of a smiling woman and a starry-eyed baby sitting on Marcus's desk. "Is that your girlfriend?" Kieran asks. There was a woman Marcus had tended to go off on irrelevant tangents about in lecture.

Marcus beams. "My *fiancée*, Glenn," he says.

"Oh. Congratulations."

"Thank you. We're getting married in December. After this campaign is finished, one way or another. See my baby girl? Her name is Ashlynn, and you've *never* met a smarter kid."

Kieran casts an eye over at Seth's desk while Marcus rattles on about how his infant gurgles in complete sentences, just like Einstein, and is probably going to grow up to be a genius architect because she *loves* stacking blocks on top of each other. Seth is staring at his laptop with the intensity of a man who is trying so hard to look nonchalant that he can't even see what's in front of him. His face is turning pink.

Ouch, Kieran thinks. He actually feels a little bad for having brought it up, mostly because Seth—unlike the famous political figures whose personal drama Kieran used to love reading about—is a real person sitting across from him who looks kind of sad and uncomfortable. The next day, he's still feeling sympathetic, so he gets

Seth an extra pump of peppermint in his mocha. Then he's circling around the office to give everyone their ridiculous, expensive coffee, when Seth emerges from Marcus's office, looking—as usual—kind of pissed.

"Kieran," he says. "You should bring Marcus his coffee first."

Some idiot part of Kieran's brain keeps thinking that Seth is *joking* about being a) this far up his own ass and b) this far up Marcus's ass, so his automatic response is to laugh.

Then he looks at Seth's face and realizes it's never a joke with this guy. Seth is making needle eyes at him. Unfortunately, Kieran is already losing the ability to fake a friendly, obliging personality at a job he doesn't expect to last for more than a few weeks. He shrugs at the needle eyes and says, "Okay, Seth. Mind if I give you *your* coffee on the way in to see Marcus—or would that be inappropriate?"

"Go ahead," Seth says icily. He accepts his triple-shot peppermint mocha with extra peppermint.

Kieran leans in and plonks Marcus's drink on

his desk. "Sorry to keep you waiting, Your Highness."

Marcus smiles benevolently. "You don't have to serve me first, Kieran. Everyone's working hard."

Everyone except you, Kieran thinks. He goes back out to give everyone else their coffee, starting with Marie, who thanks Kieran and calls him *sweetie* in a tone that makes his skin crawl. Seth is hovering in the doorway, frowning faintly as he sips his drink. "This tastes sweeter than usual," he says. "Are you sure this is the right order?"

Kieran regrets ever feeling sorry for him. "I think so. Might've ordered a hundred shots of syrup in that one instead of ninety-nine."

Marie giggles. "Watch out, Seth! She's got a mouth on her."

Kieran stiffens, but Marie doesn't seem to notice. Neither does anyone else, for that matter. Kieran's still handing out coffees, and he can feel the appropriate time frame for him to correct Marie rapidly closing, but he can't bring himself to say anything.

For all that he has such a mouth on him, his throat closes up.

"*He's*," Seth says, loudly. "*Him*."

Kieran doesn't look around, but he hears Marie's startled acknowledgement. "Oh, excuse me, Kieran. Just a slip of the tongue."

"It's fine," Kieran mumbles. His expectations were never exactly high.

"Marie, I expect you—and everyone—to make more of an effort in the future," Seth says curtly. "None of our employees should have to wear a label to remind the rest of us what to call them, but Kieran has been, so the least we can do is get it right."

Shut up, Kieran thinks, his face burning. "It's *fine*," he says.

Seth is apparently perceptive enough to notice that he's embarrassed, and goes back into his office without another word.

Nobody says anything more than a quiet "thanks" as Kieran distributes the coffee and vanishes back to his desk. He feels Seth glance at him a few times, but doesn't pay attention; he's got an inch-high stack of data to enter that Marcus forgot about until yesterday, and a reasonable quantity of black coffee to drink.

* * *

Kieran doesn't know if he feels more resentment or gratitude toward Seth. There had been a magical moment of sheer relief when he'd heard a voice that wasn't his own reminding Marie of his pronouns. But a moment later, he'd realized how silent and uncomfortable the rest of his coworkers were, and dread had washed over him.

Now everyone is going to avoid using Kieran's pronouns at all for fear of Seth's wrath descending on them, and that'll make Kieran feel like a ghost floating around the office.

He can already feel it happening when he goes out in search of a stapler. All his coworkers go abruptly quiet and guilty at the sight of him.

Kieran curls up miserably in his desk chair and tries to focus on paperwork.

Near the end of Kieran's shift, Marcus suddenly stretches out and grabs his bag. "I've got to head out early today," he says cheerfully. "My little girl's going to a birthday party!"

Even Seth, for a moment, looks pained. Marcus never remembers to mention how long he'll be staying for the day. "All right," Seth says, with characteristic calm. "Say hello to Glenn for me."

"I'll have to bring her and Ashlynn around to

meet everyone sometime," Marcus says, pulling on his coat and adjusting his nerdy glasses. "Ash is so curious about my job!"

Then he's gone, and Kieran opens his mouth before he remembers that he's avoiding talking to Seth. "Do you think his one-year-old child is really curious about his job, or was that another gurgle he mistook for human language?"

Seth nearly smiles. After a second, he manages to smother that glimmer of positivity with a disapproving stare. "*Excuse* me?"

"Never mind," Kieran says, and goes back to categorizing poll results.

Most people's shifts ended a while ago, and most of the workforce has shuffled off. Conversations have ended and the sun is setting, leaving the office quiet except for the clicking of keyboards, the hum of the fan, and the breeze rustling papers on Kieran's desk.

Seth stops typing suddenly.

"I apologize if I put you on the spot earlier," he says.

Kieran isn't prepared to respond to an apology. "It's fine."

"I'm happy to talk to the other employees individually about the importance of respecting your pronouns."

The importance. That's a first.

"They're getting used to it," Kieran mutters. "Don't make me the most hated guy in the office."

Seth goes uncomfortably silent.

"I talk a lot," Kieran says. He does. He likes the sound of his own voice. He just knows what it sounds like to other people. High, affected—*girly*. It's the *Mean Girls* voice he cultivated in high school. "I'm shrill, you know. It tricks their brains. I can tell them to call me *he*, but I can't change what's going on in their heads when I talk to them."

"Don't make excuses for us," Seth says quietly. "You can expect better here."

Kieran glances sidelong at him and accidentally makes eye contact. Seth gives him a faint, sincere smile. Kieran clears his throat, startled. "Yeah?"

"Yes."

Why would you do that for me? Kieran wants to ask, but the question won't take shape in his mouth. Instead he mutters, "Okay, Mister This-Coffee-Is-Too-Sweet-Does-It-Have-Extra-Peppermint."

Seth's brows knit together. "I didn't say you could get my coffee order wrong."

"I didn't get it *wrong*."

"In that case, the barista did, because I could taste—"

Kieran groans. "You looked like you were having a rough day, so I asked for extra syrup. I figured you wouldn't mind more of a good thing, since you get the most oversugared shit in the office anyway." He probably shouldn't swear in front of his superiors, but his shift ended two minutes ago, so technically this is off the record. Ish. "Sorry. Won't happen again."

Seth looks stuck between confusion and disapproval. It's not a good look on him. It makes him look older—something about the crinkles around his mean, glinty eyes. "I—" He swivels his chair around to face Kieran. "I appreciate the thought. But it upsets the balance of the flavors."

"Oh." That's probably the most reasonable thing Seth has said today. "So ask for more chocolate as well?"

"If I'm having a rough day," Seth says, "chances are what I need is an extra shot of espresso. But I'll ask, thank you."

Kieran throws him a lazy salute and bows his head over his desk. He keeps working as an excuse not to look up.

"Your shift is over," Seth says.

"There's twenty pages left."

"I'll finish up here. Go home."

"I don't have anything better to do at home."

"You don't get paid overtime."

"I don't get *paid*."

Seth sighs. "Give me half of the stack."

Kieran is pretty sure Seth has his own work to do, but he hands him the ten pages, and by their powers combined, the work goes remarkably fast. In fifteen minutes, the last numbers have been entered and Seth runs a few dozen papers through the shredder while Kieran stuffs his laptop into his bag.

"Good work today," Seth says.

"Thanks. See you—" Not *tomorrow*, though that catches on his tongue for a moment. He doesn't have another shift until the weekend. "Uh, next time. Have a good night?"

Maybe it's just that Kieran sounds a lot less resentful than usual, but Seth looks startled, and gives him a small, unpracticed smile. "Good night," Seth says.

While Kieran is meandering to the bus stop, it occurs to him that maybe Seth is so set on correcting the office workers on his pronouns because *Marcus* cares about trans stuff. Marcus was all excited about hiring a skinny, testosterone-free trans guy straight out of college, but Marcus doesn't have the personality or the attention span to monitor how everybody uses Kieran's pronouns. So Seth sits there listening with his obnoxiously sharp hearing and making sure everybody gets it right... so Marcus's office can be the fluffy safe space he wants it to be.

Yeah, Kieran thinks, that would explain a lot.

Somehow, he's not satisfied with feeling like he solved the mystery of Seth's behavior. With a stupid little pang, he realizes he was actually kind of hoping Seth was just doing it for him.

* * *

As the launch of the new campaign website creeps closer, accompanied by some alarming funding deadlines, the work piles up on Kieran's desk. He has more to do than he has time in his shifts; everyone does. At first Kieran keeps clocking out as usual, right on the hour, but he feels weird going home to watch Netflix when he knows the job isn't done. Like it or not, he's caught a little of the energy of the workplace. Also, now that he's spending a lot more time paying attention to Heidi Norton's campaign platform, he's realizing how cool she is. She cares about raising the minimum wage and reproductive rights and a bunch of other stuff that gives Kieran a glimmer of hope to read about.

For a political science major, he's spent a long time cultivating a feeling of inevitability and despair about who gets elected, but being in the trenches makes it hard to feel as powerless. He wants Heidi Norton in office, and with each shift, it feels like he's nudging the universe a bit more in that direction.

He doesn't tell Jillian about his newfound investment, because she'd be unbearably smug.

He does, however, start taking the job seriously. At first he hangs around fifteen minutes past the end of his shift, then thirty. Seth is always there, and Kieran gets used to the quiet solidarity of working long into the evening with him. Heck, it's not like he has anything better to do.

One night, when Marcus is flitting between desks out in the main room and trying to keep the cogs of the enterprise moving, Seth leans across to Kieran's desk. "Kieran. What time does your shift end?"

"Ten minutes ago," Kieran says. "What do you want? Blood, sweat, or tears?"

"I think Marcus is going to need another coffee. His usual. Do you mind running to the café?"

Kieran stretches, savoring the idea of a walk. "Nope. Company card?"

Seth tosses it across to his desk with minimum suspicion. Progress.

The usual barista is startled to see Kieran in so late, but appreciates the tips. Kieran wishes she didn't call him *sweetie*, but he puts up with it, like he puts up with the weird customers who call him *baby* and *miss* at his other job. He returns to the office to find the lights on but the desks empty, except for Jake—the web developer, who has his own pot of coffee sitting half-drunk next to his computer—and Seth.

Seth looks up as Kieran walks in and frowns

at the sight of the coffee in his hands. "Ah. You're back."

"Where's Marcus?" Kieran asks.

Seth massages his temples. "He went home. Apparently his daughter has a cold."

Kieran can't even fault him for that, really. Sick babies are probably scary even for normal, well-collected parents, which Marcus is not. "What now?"

"I'm going to finish what I can tonight," Seth says. "The new site needs testing." He blinks when Kieran sets a cup on his desk. "What's this?"

"Dude, it's a triple-shot peppermint mocha, like it is every single day."

"I didn't ask for anything," Seth says, doing his best to look irritated by Kieran's consideration.

"Yeah, but you always stay late if he does," Kieran says, nodding over at Marcus's desk. "And, uh. Even if he runs off."

Seth glares at his coffee cup. Either Kieran's imagining things, or he's blushing at the mere implication of Marcus. Kieran wants to shake him. "Well—thank you. I don't usually have caffeine after six."

Kieran pats him on the back. Seth's shoulder is bony and warm, and something about noticing that feels too intimate, so Kieran stuffs his hands into his pockets and backs off. "Just think of it as slamming an energy drink before a final."

Seth picks up his coffee and takes a prim sip. He doesn't say anything about the shoulder pat, which probably means it was only weird and intimate for one of them. "It's been a long time since I had a final," Seth says.

"No kidding," Kieran says. "What are you? Fifty?"

Seth sneers. "You're too kind, young man."

Young man. A faint warmth settles in Kieran's chest, and he looks away, grinning. "So... sixty?"

"Thirty-five, thank you."

"And you don't look a day older. Think I can have Marcus's drink?"

"I don't see why not." Seth glances after him as Kieran goes and settles at his desk again. "You can go home, Kieran."

"Split whatever work you've got halfsies with me," Kieran says, waving an inviting hand. "You'll be here till midnight otherwise."

"I'm going to be awake past midnight anyway," Seth mutters, with the contempt of an eighty-year-old.

"Whatever. Let me help out and you can hurry home to..." Kieran has no idea what Seth goes home to at night, actually. He envisions loneliness. A clean, well-kept void. "Your loving wife and children?" he suggests.

Seth makes a muffled noise that's almost a laugh, like he knows it's a joke. "All right. If you can test the links on the new website, that would be helpful."

Kieran slurps at Marcus's gross caramel syrup drink and gets to work on the website. There are only about nine hundred broken links, so that's great. "So what's her name?"

"Marian," Seth says. "And my loving child is Dragon."

Kieran stares at him.

Seth catches his look with a raised eyebrow. "Marian was my wife. We separated years ago, of course. And we never had children."

"Dragon?"

"My cat."

"Oh." Kieran feels the embarrassed recoil that comes of accidentally asking a more private question than he meant to. Seth doesn't seem sad enough to merit an apology, but Kieran doesn't want to leave the subject there, hanging in the air. "Hey, it's probably good for the campaign. If you *and* Marcus had kids, you'd both be out every day with a kid's birthday party or soccer practice or whatever."

Seth gives a tiny sigh. Acknowledgement, Kieran thinks.

"I feel for him," Seth says. "It must be hard to come to work at all. I think he'd spend every moment at home with his daughter if he could."

"He might as well bring her to the office," Kieran says, draining the last of the caramel monstrosity.

"I don't know that a crying infant would increase anyone's productivity," Seth says, and now the curl at the corner of his mouth is at least seventy-percent smile. "Did you finish that drink already?"

"I had to get it over with," Kieran says, gagging slightly. "How can you stand that much syrup?"

"I don't know. I labor through it, somehow." Seth gives him that sideways look. "Are you working?"

"Yes! *And* I'm logging errors. Check the bug tracker if you don't believe me."

"I believe you."

The silence between them is comfortable now, when they settle into it. Kieran keeps sneaking looks at Seth, trying to decide if he's just striking or actually really handsome. He does have a bit of a permafrown going on, but other than that, Kieran likes his face: high, sharp cheekbones and a long swoop of a nose, skeptical eyebrows, and bright brown eyes. Seth doesn't seem to notice him staring. Despite the triple-shot of caffeine, he looks tired.

"Have the other employees been working on your pronouns?" Seth asks after a while.

Oh, are we going to talk about this? Kieran thinks sourly. "They've been avoiding them."

"Hmm," Seth says. "I was hoping they'd get better over time. I know Marie is struggling, so I've been trying to keep an eye on her. Marcus slipped up the other day, but I told him—"

"Can we *not?*"

That's all Kieran can muster, for a moment.

Seth pauses, staring at him, startled and expectant. Kieran swallows and fumbles for politer words. "You know—like—if you get a splinter or something, it doesn't hurt until you fucking press on it?"

"Ah," Seth says.

Kieran keeps his eyes fixed on his screen, hunching his shoulders. "I know people make mistakes. I hear them. I don't need a report of all the other times it happens. And I don't really want to talk about it unless you've got a great plan for making sure nobody ever misgenders me again." It occurs to Kieran that he's, as usual, probably out of line. "Sorry if that's blunt. But it stresses me out."

"No. I apologize." Seth hesitates. "I've only handled changing pronouns for friends before, never employees. I'm not entirely sure how to manage it." Another pause, and Kieran doesn't know what to say. He's busy thinking, *friends? Seth has trans friends?* Maybe he isn't just doing this for Marcus's sake. "Your comfort is the most important thing. If I've made you uncomfortable, I've mishandled things."

"It's fine," Kieran says. "I just don't want it to be a big deal."

"I understand."

"Yeah?"

"Well, I empathize."

"Yeah."

Kieran wishes he had something to do with his hands besides type, something to do with his eyes besides work, because then it would be easier to distract himself. So much for the comfortable quiet.

Apparently Seth is aware of the atmosphere in the room, because he quietly asks, "What did you study in college?"

"Political science. I met Marcus in Poli-Sci 101."

"How was he? As a teacher?"

"Terrible," Kieran says, before his brain can catch up with his mouth.

Seth frowns at him. "That's a little harsh."

"Er. Don't tell him I said that. And hear me out. He was great for getting this internship, and he was the nicest prof I ever had. But he forgot half of what he was supposed to lecture about, every day. Then he'd forget to rewrite the tests to take out all the things we didn't cover in class. He fixed people's grades when they complained about the exams, but then he'd do it again."

Seth purses his lips. "That does sound frustrating."

"He *was* nice."

"He is very nice."

Seth is back to staring at his computer. But he's got that look again, like he isn't really seeing it.

Kieran purses his lips. They've talked about Kieran's transness. Maybe they can talk about the other thing. "At least he's handsome, right?"

Seth's head snaps up. "What?"

"He's a good-looking guy. In the nerdy way."

"I hadn't noticed," Seth mumbles, running his fingers around his collar.

"Oh, come on. I get that all the straights don't pay attention, but—"

Seth cuts him off, loudly. "I *don't* know what made you think that was an appropriate topic," he says, voice sharp and angry. Kieran snaps his mouth shut in surprise. "It isn't."

Kieran can't quite wrap his head around the sudden change in Seth's tone, from practically amiable to frigid. He's baffled. And kind of hurt. "Wait, so—I was assigned female at birth, and that's okay to talk about, but your crush on our boss isn't appropriate?"

"Excuse me?" The color in Seth's face is seriously intense. "This is a professional setting, Kieran."

Okay, so maybe he did cross a line. *Maybe*. But the possibility makes him bluster harder. "Yeah, that's why Marcus shows up in a T-shirt every day and blows off work to plan parties for his toddler. And that's why we're here chatting about my pronouns!"

"None of that is an excuse for bringing up any employee's *sex* life or for reading into the interactions between me and—" Seth fumbles his way free of that sentence without quite finishing it. He slaps his laptop closed and rises, grabbing his laptop sleeve. "That's enough. I can finish the work later. Go home, Kieran."

"Who said anything about sex?" Kieran protests. "I didn't say—"

"*Enough*," Seth snaps. "Go. Home. And for future reference, I do expect a better grasp of workplace etiquette from someone Marcus *personally* selected to intern here, even if they have such an apparently poor opinion of him."

Kieran stands, shaking, but he can't really think of anything else to say.

He shoves his shit in his satchel and leaves the office.

3.

He'd just been miserably sure, for half a second, that somebody might get it. That somebody else might be as exposed as he is every fucking day. That somebody else might be wearing a glaringly obvious secret on his skin. He thought maybe that was a thing he and Seth had in common: an inability to hide whatever made them different, whatever made them *queer*.

Failing that, he'd at least been sure they were getting along. Maybe his standards for "getting along" are kind of low.

He's embarrassed to admit that he got his hopes up, even to Jillian, so he complains to her about Marcus and pretends that's why he's upset.

When he's done being mad, it occurs to him

to worry that Seth might tell Marcus something. Probably Seth would leave out the part about his own crush on Marcus and just say how Kieran was behaving inappropriately for the office and said he was a shit professor. That would probably do it.

He shows up to his next shift unsure of whether he's about to be asked to leave. Instead, all that greets him is Marcus's usual cheery grin and Seth's familiar chilly indifference. Well, it's chillier than before. Seth doesn't look at him except to give occasional orders, and doesn't even lift his head when Kieran talks to him.

Fucking asshole. His relief quickly drains away to irritation.

"The mood in here seems a bit low today," Marcus says gently. "Kieran, why don't you get some donuts with the coffee? There's a great donut shop a few blocks down, if you wouldn't mind going out of your way."

Seth doesn't say anything, but he lets out an audible sigh.

"Sure," Kieran says. That gets him about a half hour of freedom before he's back in the office, chewing on some (very good, very fresh) donuts and logging infinite bugs on the campaign website.

Marcus is, unsurprisingly, also terrible at using the bug tracker. He has a habit of thinking everything is perfect long before it's fixed.

Eating donuts doesn't improve Seth's personality. But there is something heartwarming about watching Seth scowl at the sugar stuck to his fingers and trying to subtly lick it off.

He catches Kieran watching and glares at him.

Kieran quickly averts his eyes, but he feels a strange jolt of relief. Then he realizes it's because it's the first time Seth has given him that nasty look all day—and he'd gotten used to receiving it about five times an hour. The bland silence is infinitely worse.

It's weird to realize that maybe Seth hasn't been that annoyed with him all along. Maybe his face just does that. Maybe the pissy glare is Seth being amiable.

What a shitty way to find out.

* * *

"Welcome to Beefy Burgers," Kieran says. "What can I get for you?"

The customer is probably like nineteen, or a precocious high school senior, but he clearly thinks he's hot shit. To his credit, he's cute, in a wannabe frat boy way. He's got long eyelashes and a cocky smile, and for a second Kieran genuinely grins back at him.

Then the kid fully leans on the counter, resting his elbows on the back of the register, and stares at Kieran's chest.

It's a sharp, nasty reminder that he's not wearing his binder, that he's in girl mode, and that this is not the kind of flirtation Kieran would like it to be. The familiar gut-stab of dysphoria drags him back down to earth.

"I guess I'll take a burger," the kid says, smirking.

Kieran has heard this intro too many times to be drawn into a playful guessing game as to what kind of burger this kid wants. He says, as blandly as possible, "The basic burger? Do you want fries with that?"

The kid looks up, and whatever he sees in Kieran's eyes changes his attitude from greasy to affronted in about two seconds. "No," he mumbles. "Just the burger."

He makes a point of not tipping, which is hilarious, since it's fast food and nobody expects him to tip. But Kieran gets the message. The kid might as well say "Fuck you for not flirting back."

* * *

Kieran doesn't really talk to anyone, not even Jillian, about his day job. Mostly because even Jillian, with all her optimism, hates being presented with a problem she can't fix. She can't get him a new job where the customers don't think he's a girl, because that's any job, every job. She knows better than to try to tell him that it'd be easier somewhere else.

Honestly, flipping burgers isn't so bad. The problem is people.

"Flipping burgers" is actually Kieran's shorthand for "working the front register in fast food hell." He's not the absolute best at wearing a fake smile or pretending to be excited about taking people's orders, but one thing does give him staying power: he's really good at not caring. His managers have never exactly declared him their favorite employee, but they do praise his attitude, which is funny because no one else ever has. And it's all because Kieran has never burst into tears over a customer screaming at him, never complained about kids spilling their soda all over the counter and all over his shoes, never had much of a reaction at all to customers getting up in his face and sneering *sweetie, girl, bitch.*

In his head, he's always watching Netflix.

Sometimes he takes a count of how many times he gets misgendered in a day, just to have the statistics, even if he's never liked math very much. It's not exactly fair, since he's not out at the job, but it's also not like anyone has ever asked him what his pronouns are. He told Jillian about the counting once and she looked so sad that he made a silent vow to never mention it to her again.

He has a running list of his least favorite kinds of customers. Condescending old people are definitely up there, casual bigots are pretty bad, and worst of all are the guys who hit on him. They're the worst because, in addition to being gross, some of them are actually his type—or they would be if they weren't hitting on him at work. They're the worst because it's harder to space out when he's talking to a hot guy, harder to crush down the mixture of intrigue and nausea that hits him when a guy who thinks he's a girl starts flirting with him across the register. Usually he just goes home and forgets about it, or calls Jillian and babbles about nothing until the sick feeling in his stomach resolves. Tonight, though, he's got a shift at the campaign office. One of his coworkers accidentally dumps mop water on his shoes on the way back from a cleanup, so Kieran has to sprint home for dry socks in between jobs. He misses his bus. By the time he jogs up to the office, he's half an hour late and so out of breath from running in his binder that he doubles over in the elevator and wheezes all the way to the top floor.

"You're late," Seth observes, when he comes in. Marcus is nowhere to be seen.

"I got held up at my other job," Kieran says, more sharply than he really should. He tosses his bag on his desk and sinks into his chair, still red in the face and breathing a little hard. The last thing he wants to deal with is Seth disapproving of him, mostly because he's actually a little upset about being late and doesn't need the external condemnation. When Seth keeps looking at him, Kieran bristles and jerks his head up. "I'm sorry—"

"Are you feeling sick?" Seth interrupts.

There's none of the disapproval Kieran expected in his voice. There's measured but genuine concern, instead, and Kieran is momentarily thrown off guard. He should probably be alarmed that he looks bad enough for Seth to comment on it, but he's... distracted.

Kindness makes his intense eyes soften into something attentive but careful, like he can see that Kieran is fraying at the seams. It makes Seth's face go from sharp and intimidating to sympathetic, calm, and really handsome.

Kieran's stomach twists, not as unpleasantly as with his customer earlier. Still, he can't handle this feeling right now.

Seth watches him, waiting for an answer, while Kieran wrestles his way back from *uncomfortably attracted to frigid supervisor*. "No," he manages. "I'm fine. I just ran up here."

"Is everything all right at your other job?" Seth asks, delicately.

Kieran nods, kind of mechanically, and adds, "Just a long day. I can stay late to make up for it."

"No, that's... not necessary." Seth looks awkward. "I apologize. You've always been on time, so it's not an issue. I was just surprised."

"It was either be late or come in smelling like a mop bucket."

"Ah." Seth offers him a faint smile. "Well, you made the right choice."

Kieran finds himself smiling back, wishing the flush in his cheeks would go away. It's definitely outstayed its welcome, and he doesn't need to broadcast to the world the weird moment he's having where Seth's face is nice and extra hot. "Uh, thanks. Good. So—got any work for me?"

"Yes," Seth says, almost too quickly. He looks away. "Yes. I was wondering if you could try your hand at a draft of the new campaign text messages—we need to cover a few upcoming events. I'll send you the details."

Kieran relaxes into his chair. "Awesome. I can do that."

It's good, distracting work, and it makes Kieran feel useful because he's more knowledgeable than anyone in the office about texting. Plus, it feels like actually creating something, and he's a little flattered that Seth trusts him enough to let him do it.

Unfortunately, being flattered by Seth is exactly the kind of thing he needs to be distracted from. He's almost relieved when Marcus wafts in, apologizing for being late. When Marcus is around, Kieran can usually trust Seth to be distracted.

If only the same could be said for Marcus. After a little while of rearranging things on his desk, picking at a sticker on his monitor, and turning up the fan pointed at his chair, Marcus swivels toward Kieran. "What are you working on today?" he asks, in a tone that Kieran imagines he also uses when talking to his infant child.

"He's writing the new campaign texts," Seth says briskly.

Marcus brightens. "Fantastic!" He beams at Kieran over the top of his monitor. "That reminds me. I don't want to distract from what you're doing…"

Kieran tears his eyes away from the sentence he's been trying to cram into fewer characters for the last fifteen minutes. "What's up?"

Marcus's eyes do that obnoxious twinkling thing when he smiles. "I just wanted to say how happy I am that you've settled in. I know how much politics means to you, and how nervous you were about being able to get started in the field."

Don't do this today, Kieran thinks. *Don't do this in front of Seth.*

His stomach sinks. "I mean," he tries to say, "I wasn't really—"

"I hope this is reassuring," Marcus continues. "I don't want you to think that *anything* about you isn't suited to politics. Least of all something you can't change."

"I don't think that," Kieran mutters.

"Well, good. It broke my heart that you used to feel that way."

Normally, Kieran would just let that kind of thing slide, because Marcus has never taken the hint and been anything other than bubbly and condescending. But Seth is right there, politely pretending not to listen but clearly capable of hearing, and the idea of Seth seeing him the way Marcus does sets Kieran's teeth on edge.

"I didn't feel that way," he says. "I was just worried about how *politics* was suited to *me*."

Marcus chuckles. "Same difference," he says, and Kieran bites his tongue. "Either way, I hope the campaign is proving you wrong. I want this to give you the confidence going forward to believe that you can do anything."

Classic Marcus. *Just hate yourself less and success will find you.*

Once, *once*, during undergrad, Kieran had made the mistake of confiding in Marcus. Crying in his office, venting all his fears, the works. It hadn't really been anything to do with his wanting to confide in Marcus specifically so much as his needing someone, anyone, to talk to. Marcus had been sympathetic, concerned, and for a brief shining moment Kieran had liked him.

Except that for the rest of the school year, Marcus had brought it up at every opportunity.

It was like he'd suddenly taken it on himself to be Kieran's protective uncle. And it never seemed to matter how much Kieran didn't want to be reminded of his terrible life or treated like the world's most tragic victim—it was obvious that Marcus had never seen him the same way again. There was always a spark of pity and admiration in Marcus's eyes when he looked at Kieran that made Kieran want to scream *If you feel so bad for me, try fixing the world*.

"It's making *me* happier to be in such an inclusive workplace," Marcus adds, oblivious to Kieran's silence. "And it didn't really take that much work! All people need is someone to set a good example."

"I think we could be setting a better example," Seth says, very lightly.

Marcus looks honestly startled. "Oh?"

"Yes."

Kieran stares hard at Seth out of the corner of his eye, but Seth doesn't look back at him. Seth clears his throat and continues, "I think there are more steps we can and should take before congratulating ourselves."

Marcus scratches the back of his neck, looking embarrassed. "You think so?"

"Yes. We can discuss it later." There's an edge of finality in Seth's voice, and he looks back at his monitor, effectively closing the conversation. Marcus looks at him for a minute, then tries to catch Kieran's eye—Kieran hastily pretends to be absorbed in the text draft—and finally goes back to work. He doesn't say another word to Kieran for the rest of his shift.

Kieran tries to focus on his task, but once again he's stuck with a mixture of gratitude and misery thanks to Seth. He realizes that Seth, completely contrary to Kieran's expectations, just shut Marcus down when he was in the middle of patting himself on the back—which is more than Kieran has ever been able to do. That ought to feel awesome.

Instead he feels like the sore thumb, the office

nuisance. He feels like a renovation nobody wanted, a tacky paint job Marcus thought everyone would like even though it offends and confuses all of their sensibilities.

The truth is that people like him fine as long as he doesn't ever raise his voice and as long as Seth isn't correcting anybody for misgendering him. They don't *get* him, though; they don't really know what he is, because nobody ever bothered to tell them.

He keeps his head down over his keyboard, but doesn't get anything done beyond retyping the same sentence over and over, trying to make it snappy and failing.

It's just too much. He realizes, with an awful lurch, that it's all he can do to keep from tearing up.

Marcus slips out with a muttered excuse about checking on everyone in the main room. The moment the door closes behind him, Seth gives an audible sigh.

"I'm sorry," he says. "I realize that was putting you on the spot again, but—"

"*Please* don't pity me," Kieran says. His hands

are shaking. He drops them from the keyboard and squeezes them between his knees.

"I don't," Seth says, sounding startled. "I think you're very—"

"Don't say 'brave.'"

Seth clears his throat. "I was going to say 'accomplished.'"

Kieran isn't sure he believes him, but whatever, it's good enough. "Okay, great, because I don't want to talk about it. I just... I just want to get this draft done."

After a moment's pause, Seth says, "All right."

He leaves it there.

4.

The first thing Kieran hears when he gets to the office on Saturday is a wailing infant. He has a moment of bitter apprehension before he walks in and realizes it's coming from behind Marcus's door.

Everyone in the room is wearing headphones, and several of them glance at him with vague sympathy as he goes to join Seth and Marcus and Ashlynn in the other room.

Except Marcus isn't even there. The little girl is parked in a stroller next to his desk, screaming. Seth is hunched over next to the baby, awkwardly cooing and shaking a rattle at her.

It's the cutest and most pathetic thing Kieran has ever seen. He grins involuntarily. When Seth looks up, he frantically tries to rearrange his face into something appropriately sympathetic, but it doesn't quite work. "Uh," he coughs. "Marcus ditched you with a baby? That's harsh."

"He stepped out," Seth says coldly. "He said he thought she was crying because she's hungry."

Kieran edges closer to the stroller, which is like approaching an ambulance with its sirens blaring. Inside is a small, fairly adorable baby in bright green pajamas. Her face is twisted in fury, and she's not paying any attention to Seth's feeble rattling. She's bellowing with rage, her face squashed up. "You're probably just pissing her off."

"Would *you* like to try?"

"Yeah, as long as you don't give me any shit about having *mom instincts*." Kieran pulls Marcus's cozy office chair over by the stroller and scoops Ashlynn carefully into his arms. She stops crying with a startled, teary gurgle and glares at him in confusion. "Hi, kiddo. Give your dad a minute. Please."

"Should you be holding her?" Seth asks, leaning over with great concern.

"I have a baby brother. Got pretty used to carrying him around for my mom when she was busy."

Ashlynn's grimacing at him like she might start screaming again, but he starts rocking her back and forth and she seems to reconsider. She gives a few teary gurgles, then settles down and stares, damp-eyed, as Kieran makes faces at her. "Babies are so weird."

"Yes," Seth agrees.

"She does look smart, though."

"I was just thinking that."

Kieran glances at Seth. He's staring at the kid like... well, not like he wishes he had one, but like he wishes for *something*.

Seth catches Kieran looking and frowns.

"How long's she been screaming for?" Kieran asks.

"About half an hour."

"Uncool." Kieran jiggles Ashlynn gently. He hears the office door open and scoots back to the stroller, returning her. She starts screaming again the moment Marcus walks in, but gets quiet as soon as she's being cradled in his lap and spoon-fed baby food.

"Glenn's at a recital today," Marcus explains. "She asked if I could bring Ashlynn to meet everyone at work. I was hoping she'd sleep, but she has a real appetite these days!"

"Sure seems like it," Kieran agrees. He exchanges a look with Seth. Seth does not look good; which is to say he seems as pissy as usual, but also sad and frazzled. He keeps glancing wistfully at Marcus, then ducking his head and focusing all too hard on his work.

Which can't be easy. Even after Ashlynn is fed and appeased and resting peacefully in her stroller, Marcus keeps jingling a rattle at her and cooing and trying to get her to play with him.

Kieran has never met anyone more capable of making everyone else's work harder while doing nothing.

Kieran doesn't usually take a lunch break because his shifts are so short it's barely worth it—and definitely not one hour after arriving at work. But this is an exceptional case. "I'm gonna grab something to eat," he says, and Marcus nods with a distracted smile. "Hey—Seth. Want to come with me?"

"That's all right," Seth says faintly.

Come on, idiot. I'm giving you an out. "Are you sure? I can *hear* your stomach gurgling."

Seth eyes him. Eyes Marcus. Eyes the baby.

Kieran raises his eyebrows.

"Fine," Seth says. He rises stiffly and follows Kieran from the office.

"You looked like you could use a break," Kieran says, as they start down the stairs.

Seth sighs abruptly and straightens his tie. "I—thank you. I appreciate the concern."

Kieran swallows, feeling oddly nervous. It hadn't really occurred to him until this moment that rescuing his supervisor from their boss was kind of a strange thing to do, kind of too intimate for their relationship. They've had such a tense relationship anyway that he's not sure why he so wanted to get Seth out of that office. There's nothing to do now but roll with it, though. "What do you want for lunch, Mister Opinionated?"

"I was planning on Korean barbecue. There's a good place a few blocks down." Seth glances at him. "Any objections?"

"None at all."

Seth leads the way, steering them down the sidewalk. His hair must be slicked in place, because it doesn't move, even in the breeze that sends Kieran's blustering in every direction. Kieran's mouth feels gummy with the absence of something to say, with trapped, half-formed sentences. He keeps watching Seth instead, noticing that the crinkles around his eyes are still deep, something tense in his step. At least he doesn't seem to notice Kieran watching him; he's absorbed in whatever's going on in his brain.

The barbecue place is hot, crowded, and smells like heaven—meaty heaven. To Kieran's surprise, Seth asks for a table, not takeout. "They're busy," he says. "We might as well be sitting if we have to wait a while." The two of them cozy into a booth in a cramped corner of the restaurant. The surrounding tables are split between families having lunch together and other workers on their lunch break.

Seth pulls off his blazer and sits primly. One elegant swipe of his hair comes loose in the heat and tries to lie across his forehead. He smooths it back into place—which is a shame, because he looks more human, more touchable, when he's a little bit rumpled.

Touchable. That's apparently a place Kieran's brain is going. Great.

"Penny for your thoughts?" Seth asks.

Kieran does his best to look casual and not lustful or deeply awkward. "Uh, just wondering. Have you ever met Marcus's aunt?"

"Senator Norton?" Seth asks, blinking. "Yes. She visited the office once for the ribbon-cutting—such as it was. This office isn't terribly important."

"I figured. Marcus wouldn't last if it was."

Seth starts to look disapproving.

"Come on. I like the guy, but all he wants to do is be a stay-at-home dad. Can you imagine if the office *needed* a manager to devote all their time to it? He'd quit. Or he'd get fired."

Seth purses his lips and glances out the window, but he doesn't seem to have anything to say in Marcus's defense. "You don't believe in softening the truth, do you?"

"I believe in it. I just get tired of it. Believe me, I spend too much time not talking."

"Do you?"

"At my other job." Kieran shrugs, carding his hands through his fluffy curls, still wind rumpled. "Flipping burgers. I don't care. I tune out. Basically I pretend like I don't even exist when I'm working there."

Seth raises his eyebrows. "So you have to do the opposite in a *professional* setting?"

"Hey, it's super easy to be a robot when nobody really wants you to be anything. But Marcus was always happy when people talked in class. He got nervous lecturing alone, so even if I talked too much, he'd thank me. I figured his office would be the same way, and I'm not great at shutting up when I don't have to."

"I've noticed," Seth says.

The waiter shows up and Kieran hasn't even looked at the menu.

"Uh," he says.

"It's your first time here," Seth says. "Try the galbi."

Something about Seth ordering for him makes Kieran feel pampered. He rubs the back of his neck, face flushed. "Sure."

Then they're alone again.

Seth looks out the window for a long time. He fixes a tiny wrinkle in his shirtsleeve.

Then he runs his fingers under his collar absently and sighs. "I'm glad we're having lunch," he says.

"Uh?"

"I wanted to apologize."

Kieran's not sure what to do with his face. He frowns.

"First of all for what Marcus said the other day. I don't want us to be complacent."

"He's the one who should apologize," Kieran says. "Not you."

"Maybe so, but you have my apology." Seth steeples his fingers. "And I do feel as responsible for the environment as he is. Which is why I wish I hadn't snapped at you for bringing up how I... how I feel about him."

"Oh," Kieran says. "Uh."

"It wasn't about professionalism. It was about my own comfort. Or lack thereof." Seth doesn't look at Kieran, which is fine. "I'm afraid I don't have your ability to be so open. I don't like to discuss certain personal matters at work."

Kieran could gracefully accept his apology. Or he could open his fucking mouth, and guess which one he does. "Neither do I," he says, and even to his own ears he sounds sullen. "For some reason it always seems to come up, though."

Seth blinks at him for a moment before it dawns on him. "Ah."

"Yeah, sorry. I do get it. You'd rather not have to be queer at work."

Seth winces. "I'm not overly fond of the word 'queer', either."

"Oh."

"It's not that I don't identify with the general idea, it's more that I can't help thinking of it as..." Seth's face closes a little. "As the kind of thing boys call each other when they can't think of anything worse."

Oh. That's the kind of experience Kieran can't really identify with, since he never got much of a shot at boyhood. Although he doesn't want to, he feels a prickle of resentment. "I guess I think of it as what we called each other in college when we didn't want to use *gay* to refer to everyone who's not straight and cisgender."

Seth ducks his head. "I understand that. It doesn't bother me so much when other people talk about the community, about themselves. I suppose, since I didn't come out until I was older, I just never had much of a chance for positive associations with being *called* queer."

Kieran doesn't know what to say to that. For some reason he's never thought of Seth as being any younger than he is now. When he imagines Seth in college or high school, closeted and probably even nerdier than he is at thirty-five, getting called gay or queer for not being a jock...

Maybe he's letting his imagination run away with him, but the thought of that younger guy growing up to be withdrawn and sharp and still closeted makes Kieran's heart do a weird flip.

"That's okay," he offers. "I mean, you don't have to want to be called that."

Seth offers him a halfway smile. "I like to think so. It does feel cowardly at times."

"Cowardly?"

"Some people seem so confident in reclaiming everything that's ever been thrown at them."

Kieran shrugs, a little uncomfortable when he thinks about some of the things he's had to reclaim. Like having a voice that most people associate with mean cheerleaders in high school, not bitchy trans boys who ditched the cheering but kept the persona. Like his long hair, which he loves, but which does a great job of convincing strangers that he's a girl. Like having a roster of experiences that mean he'll never relate to guys—most guys—in the way he relates to girls, and having to wonder if that means he'll ever really be seen as a dude. Like wondering if he'll ever really be seen as a dude if he's dating another guy.

"Sometimes you have to reclaim it," he mutters. "Because it gets rubbed in your face either way."

Seth says nothing, probably because Kieran sounds unbearably sour, even to his own ears.

"Sorry," Kieran adds, after an uncomfortable pause. "Again." He still doesn't sound sorry at all. He *wants* to sound sorry. "I guess I forgot that people *can* keep that to themselves. Sometimes even if something's obvious it doesn't mean you want to talk about it. Or have it brought up at work. Every day."

To his credit, Seth looks less offended and more concerned. "I—hadn't thought about it like that. I'm sorry if I—"

"It's not you. It's my situation." He wishes he didn't sound so mean, but he can't help it. "I'm just trying to tell you where I'm coming from, because—" Kieran bites his lip. Why is he saying this to his most supportive employer ever? Why can't he just shut up? "I get that I kind of overstepped and it was shitty of me, but that's why I did. I didn't want to be the only one who was *out*. I'm sorry for making you come out to me. I'm sorry."

Kieran's surprised to realize that he means it, and for a moment the realization feels like a knot in his stomach coming undone. Except that the conversation is still happening.

Seth fiddles with his collar again, and he's gone red in the face, which is reassuring. What a terrible talk they're having. "That's all right," he says. "I can imagine it would be very uncomfortable for you. I didn't think."

"No, it's—"

They're spared from an infinite loop of apologies by the arrival of the food. The food is delicious. Kieran doesn't really notice that it's delicious until it's mostly gone, because he crams three ribs into his mouth so he can stop talking.

Seth picks at his food, though. The waiter brought tea and side dishes with the meal, and Seth nibbles at the content of the little plates as if he can't quite get around to the main course. And then he does. "Kieran," he says, and sighs. "I don't want you to have to apologize to me. I won't compare my problems to yours. All I have is terrible taste in men."

Kieran doesn't know of a graceful way to agree that Seth's life is less shitty than his (and/or that he has terrible, terrible taste). He grunts affirmatively into his galbi.

"I don't think Marcus would ever guess," Seth adds, in a quiet voice. "And I wouldn't want him to."

"I won't tell him anything."

"Thank you. I didn't think you would. I want him to feel comfortable thinking of me as a friend and colleague, not as somebody who wants more from him."

The loneliness in his voice makes Kieran frown. "God, you are *the* tragic gay man."

Seth smiles. "I'm bisexual."

"Oh." Kieran swallows his food. "I guess that's more original."

"It's crossed my mind that I'm a cliché." Seth shrugs. "I live alone with a cat."

Kieran grins, eager to change the subject. "Is this the part where you start showing me pictures of your cat?"

"Are you asking to see pictures of my cat?"

"Yeah, show me the—" *Pussy* is what his brain

wants to say, but "*kitty*" is what he manages to cough out.

Saved from his own mouth, for once.

Seth gives him an odd look, but he fishes out his phone and holds it out for Kieran to see as he scrolls through, predictably, dozens and dozens of photos of a fat and baleful black cat.

"Dragon?" Kieran asks.

"Yes." Seth smiles fondly. It's a good look on him. It deepens the wrinkles at the corners of his eyes, but in a nice way.

"Eat your lunch," Kieran mumbles, looking away, because his mouth wants to smile back.

* * *

Seth pays for the food, over Kieran's weak objections—like hell he's actually gonna *argue* with someone buying him lunch—and they're on their way. They get coffee on the way back to the office, and Seth insists on sitting for a moment. He's really embraced this whole *skipping out on work* thing.

They grab drinks and a table in the corner, and Seth keeps looking at him. "What's up?" Kieran asks.

Seth sips at his usual peppermint monstrosity. "Can I say something?"

"Yeah? Go for it."

"I don't mean this as an insult."

"Great start."

Seth sighs, pinching the bridge of his nose. "It's only an observation. Kieran, you're very good at this job. Very organized. Very quick to learn."

"*Ouch*. The truth hurts."

Seth needles him with a look. "*But*—you aren't taking it seriously. With the attitude you bring, I get the impression that you wouldn't mind if we fired you."

Kieran's first instinct is to protest, but why bother? "Well, uh—"

"I'm not saying that because I plan on firing you. I just don't understand."

"Can *I* say something?"

"Of course."

Kieran squares his shoulders. "It's because I have a hard time thinking of it as a real job. I mean, the work's real, but I don't see myself in politics. I hate to disappoint Marcus, but I don't. Also, it's not paying anything. Marcus offered me the internship, so I took it. It's good resume material, but not good enough to be fake for."

Seth frowns. "The lack of pay is a fair point. But what about it isn't *real*?"

"My chances of ever getting people to take me seriously?"

"I take you seriously," Seth says, exasperated. "So does Marcus."

"Marcus thinks I'm *brave* for getting out of bed in the morning. He doesn't take me seriously. He takes my *problems* seriously."

He expects Seth to defend Marcus, but instead Seth's brow furrows and he nods. "Well, I never thought I'd make it anywhere either," he says. "But here I am."

"Is this where you wanna be?"

"It's somewhere." Seth fixes him with a look. "Is this job where you want to be?"

"I guess? Theoretically?"

Seth lets out a patient sigh. "Theoretically."

"I mean, yeah. I graduated college and got my fancy internship. And I've got my burger-flipping gig to support it."

Seth just looks at him like he can hear Kieran's confidence waver, and for the first time since walking in to the internship, Kieran feels himself shrinking under that stare.

I don't feel like I'm anywhere, he wants to say. The restaurant, with its shitty customers and the management that doesn't even try not to misgender him, is the only part of his life that feels real. It's the part that's every bit as shitty as he expects the world to be. Of course, it's also the part that pays rent.

There's nothing he can do about it. Because who he *is* means that no matter what, any kind of success will only set him up for being seen, being dissected. He already walks into his dream internship and feels a dozen pairs of eyes fix on him as their owners desperately try to remember, *Oh yeah, this is the girl I have to pretend is a boy.* Only if he does something bigger, it won't just be the twelve people he hands coffee to. It'll be the city. The state. The country. Everybody staring at him and picking him apart and wondering what he is.

It's way better to cut himself off from the possibility of success. Make a token effort and squander what opportunity he has so he can say that he tried and failed—he wasn't cut out for it. So he can re-sign himself to flipping burgers.

"Are you all right?" Seth asks, his voice uncharacteristically soft.

Kieran's stomach feels like it's full of hot lead. For once, the blunt, honest answer sticks in his throat. He wants to say he's fine, but tears fuzz at the corners of his eyes when he tries to say so. The silence between them stretches out too long for him to just dismiss the question.

"Not really," he chokes.

Seth doesn't say anything, but he's watching when Kieran glances at him. No hint of a glare or annoyance or anything, but there's no pity, either. Just calm concern. Maybe he's seen people melt down over coffee before and it's not going to be a big deal to him if Kieran does now. That feels like permission.

"Look, I..."

Kieran lets it out, in careful, clipped sentences so people sitting at tables nearby won't notice that he's on the verge of crying, in language so detached that he could be talking about someone else. In a quiet voice, not the voice he uses to mouth off at his superiors, not the way he talks to his friends, but maybe the way he'd talk to someone who could help. He tells Seth everything he felt in college when Marcus would treat him with admiring pity, everything he feels when Marie pauses for a long, awkward moment to restructure a sentence around avoiding his pronouns. Everything that looms in his mind when he imagines the future.

It takes half an hour. He's wondering if it's appropriate or okay to mention that it's hard to breathe sometimes when he's binding his chest in the baking heat of that top-floor office, when Seth's phone chimes.

Seth jumps and brings it to his ear. "Hello? Oh, yes. Yes, sorry, there was—quite a long line. Some kind of lunchtime rush. We'll be back soon. Goodbye."

Kieran glances at his phone and realizes they've been gone for close to an hour and a half. He scrubs his eyes. "Shit. We're on the clock."

"Unfortunately, yes." Seth gets up. "I'm sorry. I should head back. If you'd like to go home, you're welcome to."

"Huh?" Kieran stands, realizing how shaky he feels. It's not the caffeine, as much as he'd like to blame it for his hands trembling. "Nah, I should..."

"Kieran. You've never missed a shift, and you've worked late at least a dozen times. Nobody will begrudge you taking the day off. And Ashlynn was crying again when Marcus called. I doubt it's going to be a relaxing shift." The way Seth speaks, it's all so perfectly reasonable.

"Yeah," Kieran finds himself saying. "Okay. I'll, uh... I'll come in for some extra hours some other time. Could you tell Marcus I was sick or something, not that I'm—" *Having some kind of disproportionate emotional collapse because somebody asked if I was okay?*

"Of course," Seth says. He sees Kieran out to the curb, and that's where they go their separate ways, Kieran to the subway and Seth to the office. Seth catches his arm before Kieran can leave. "If you'd like to talk about this again, you can. Don't worry about being on the clock. You do more work in a shift than Marcus does in the average work week."

He smiles. Kieran is startled by it, only used to seeing this particular smile directed wistfully toward Marcus. It's nice. He smiles back, almost too big. "Now you're talking."

"Don't tell him I said that," Seth says.

"Your secret's safe with me."

Seth lets go, and Kieran rubs his arm as he walks

to the subway, trying to keep the feeling of Seth's careful grip.

Oddly, he feels better. He's all cried out, and he's relieved for having dumped the emotion somewhere other than on Jillian or his supportive, long-suffering collection of stuffed animals. His possibly shitty future seems more real and shitty than ever, but at least he knows, now, why he felt scared.

Admittedly, he spends the next six hours watching cooking dramas on Netflix and eating an entire pint of ice cream, but that's his standard self-care routine.

5.

The lunch date with Seth is the start of a huge problem.

Kieran feels a little guilty about how startled and happy Jillian is when he agrees to go see a movie with her. He's not usually *that* bad at leaving his house, but thanks to his jobs, he's been pretty awful lately, and he buys her dinner afterward to apologize. She bounces in her seat all through the meal, chattering about a new girl she's seeing, and Kieran is a little surprised himself at how easy it is to smile along with her. It's amazing how much he *doesn't* feel like a lifeless loser in comparison to her, for once.

Then she asks, carefully, "So how's the internship?"

"Oh. Uh, pretty good."

Jillian narrows her eyes at him. "Details?"

Kieran knows she expects him to start with the juiciest parts, but for a moment he almost doesn't want to admit to them. It feels too weird, too good. But Jillian is already staring him down, and he's never been able to hide anything from her. "I had lunch with Seth?"

"*What?* When?"

"Like a week ago."

Her eyes flash. "And you didn't tell me? Why was this? Where did you go? Is he still weird?"

"Well..." Kieran rests his chin in one palm, embarrassed but savoring the suspense. "I sort of cried all over him."

Jillian gasps and grabs his other hand. "Tell me this story right now."

Kieran can't resist a good audience, even if that particular lunch meeting still mortifies him as much as it was good, validating, and probably necessary. He tells Jillian everything, minus a few details about how hot Seth looked while he was coaching Kieran through his emotional breakdown, and then spills on into the story of the awkward but cool week since.

"He doesn't bring the lunch thing up ever," Kieran says, "but he's not, like, sweeping it under the rug. Every time I mention something at my other job he just *listens*. He doesn't give me any shit for complaining about my customers or try to get me to feel better about it. He keeps correcting people on my pronouns so I'm almost not thinking about it, like, I know he'll take care of it. And since the election is getting closer, there's a lot more to do, so he keeps giving me real work. Letting me take stuff off his plate. *And* he's been letting me get him coffee that doesn't have peppermint in it, just to spice it up, which is cool because I've never met anybody who cared so much about syrup flavors..."

Jillian holds up her hand to stop him. "Babe," she says, "I'm really not sure I understand what the problem is?"

Kieran blinks. "Huh?"

"You keep talking about Seth and I keep wanting to say 'Congratulations, kiddo! That's awesome!' but you sound kind of mad about it."

"Well—" Mad isn't quite the right word. Frustrated. Kieran is frustrated. And yeah, everything he's said out loud to Jillian is pretty overwhelmingly positive.

The fact is, though, that Kieran can't talk about him without getting... animated.

"It sounds like your job is going better," Jillian says carefully, "and your supervisor is also great, so—"

"He *is* great," Kieran mumbles. "That's the problem."

"Ohhh," Jillian says. "Kieran. Are you mad because he's cute?"

"Check, please."

* * *

The other part of the problem is that Kieran resents Marcus. He always has. From the beginning, Marcus's attitude annoyed him; it was useful, but still obnoxious, when he realized that Marcus would put up with Kieran's shit as long as he never outright admitted to being lazy and apathetic. At least Kieran no longer has a grade riding on Marcus's good graces, but now there's another problem: he's irrationally irritated by the fact that Marcus has Seth, a reasonably hot, eagerly devoted bisexual guy, mooning over him and doesn't even have the decency to notice. Like, how hard is it to tell when a guy is uncomfortably (and *visibly*) turned on by your bare arms?

It's not that Marcus isn't attractive, but he's so incredibly dense and otherwise annoying that Kieran can't understand what Seth sees in him. The nicer Seth is to Kieran—to both of them—the more annoyed Kieran gets. "You could do better, y'know," he says, after Marcus goes home one night.

Seth shoots him a sidelong glance, but he doesn't even muster up a glower, even though Kieran is trash-talking his crush again. How times have changed. "There you go again," he says. "Trying to get fired."

Fair enough. The truth is, Kieran feels comfortable talking to Seth, even if it's stuff he probably shouldn't say. "Hey, this is off the record. Man to man."

"All right," Seth says. "Explain. How could I do better?"

"I dunno, you could swing by the nearest gay bar and pick up literally anyone."

"Marcus is a PhD candidate with a stable job and the ability to hold down a relationship."

"Yeah, *with somebody else.*"

"That still gives him an edge over some of us," Seth says lightly, and Kieran remembers that he's divorced. Not, presumably, because of any lack of attraction to women.

He doesn't feel like it would be nice to admit that he's remembering that, so instead he puffs up his chest and says, "Are you saying I can't keep a guy happy?"

Seth laughs faintly. "I didn't mean you."

Well, fair enough. If they're going to go there. "You can't be that bad. You still deserve better."

"I don't tend to think that anybody deserves a relationship."

"I meant better in general."

Seth gives him an odd look. "Thank you," he says.

"Hey, guys at the gay bar aren't that bad."

"Which gay bar is that?"

"You want a recommendation? Aiden's is pretty cool. More of a club than a bar, though." And the owner happens to be a big butch trans guy, which is half the reason Kieran always feels safe there. The other half is that he had an amazing one-night stand in a gender-neutral restroom at

Aiden's once, and going back there—even just to dance—always feels like afterglow.

Not that he needs to tell Seth any of that. "I'll think about it," Seth says. He clearly doesn't mean it. Kieran doesn't push; hot or not, crush or not, he probably shouldn't invite his supervisor to a nightclub.

Kieran's shift is eight minutes over and he's getting ready to clear out when Jake, their long-suffering website guy, leans into the room. "Hey, folks? Got a problem."

"What?" Seth asks, with weary resignation.

"Something blew up when I migrated the site over to the new server. The pages are mostly intact, but a bunch of data got scrambled. I'm guessing we've got all of it backed up somewhere, but I dunno where. Marcus always sends me whatever I need, so I don't dip into your organizational folders much. I took the site down, but if we're gonna have it live tomorrow, I'm gonna need some help figuring out what's missing." He pauses, and then with the reluctant sympathy of someone who already works harder than everyone else in the office, says, "Sorry."

"That's all right," Seth says, firmly unruffled. "Kieran, could you…?"

"Roll up my sleeves and slave away long into the night?"

"Exactly."

"Yeah, boss."

"Thank you."

Kieran makes sure to gripe as he gets settled back in at his desk, but secretly he's pleased; staying late at the office is more fun than staying at home with Netflix. Specifically, being around Seth—goading him, watching his face get all scrunchy and annoyed at the work, listening to him talk—is more fun than anything.

Seth quickly assesses which pages on the site are in the direst need and assigns them to the two of them. Kieran glances at the clock. Eight thirty p.m. And he's thrilled to still be at the office. Maybe he is cut out for this shit after all.

Or maybe, his traitor brain whispers, *you really enjoy Seth's company.*

"Does Dragon miss you when you stay late?" he asks.

Seth laughs softly. "More like she's furious with

me. However late I get home, I'm up for another hour apologizing to her."

"Wow. What a needy baby. Hey, you got any wine under your desk?"

"Do I have *what*?"

"Wine. Y'know, for celebrating after we're done here."

"I don't drink at work."

Kieran snorts. "Whatever. You probably don't drink ever."

"I *do* drink. When it's appropriate."

"Okay, where and when? Home alone with your cat?"

Seth looks annoyed, which probably means *yes*. "At bars. Occasionally."

Okay, Kieran *shouldn't* invite his supervisor out, but the opportunity is right there. They haven't had a good talk since Kieran got all weepy on Seth, and Kieran's kind of craving another conversation. "In that case, you wanna get a drink afterwards? Because I'm not gonna want coffee after this, but I could really go for a big fruity girl drink."

"I keep thinking that you're too young to drink," Seth says, carefully.

"Dude, I graduated college. I'm twenty-three. I've been boozing it for years."

"Yes, well, for *me* it's been a decade and a half."

"Is that a no on the drinking?"

Seth looks pained. "It's not a no. As long as we're done before midnight."

Kieran spends a few precious minutes researching the nearest nice bar; he'd love to take Seth to Aiden's or another crowded gay club, just to see the look on his buttoned-up face, but on the other hand, Kieran doesn't wanna ruin his life. So a classy, quiet bar it is.

Then he gets to work, determined to power through the data before midnight.

Seth seems startled by his work ethic, especially when they finish at a quarter to eleven. Jake is overwhelmingly grateful and thanks both of them profusely, and Kieran is so pleased with the time they've made that he doesn't even care when Jake stumbles over his pronouns. Seth, though, draws himself up like he's preparing to defend Kieran's honor. Kieran pats his arm and pulls him toward the door, because honestly, he doesn't give a shit about pronoun quibbles right now.

He texts Jillian—*taking him out for*

drinks??—and stuffs his phone into his pocket, grinning when it buzzes almost immediately with her incredulous reply.

"I was thinking of ways we could make the office more comfortable for you," Seth says, distracting Kieran from his phone. "I was thinking of some kind of mandatory training for the rest of the staff. Most of them haven't received any kind of LGBT safe-spaces training. What do you think?"

Kieran clears his throat, startled and feeling the shock of unexpected warmth. He clears his throat, trying to sound nonchalant. "That would be cool, I guess. I don't want it to be a big deal."

"It shouldn't be. If we make it a matter of fact, then it should seem like a simple social convention to follow. Marcus and I would enforce the policy, of course."

It's kind of hard not to want to kiss Seth when he's being unassumingly competent and *good*.

"I feel..." Kieran's throat is all gummy again. "I feel weird. Having all this for me. I feel like everyone's going to hate me for making them go to all that trouble."

"It isn't just for you, Kieran. I hope you aren't the only trans person this campaign ever employs.

Or the only person whose gender could be misunderstood. It's a matter of policy. Of making sure all our employees are treated well. Besides, it could change how they all treat other people in their lives who don't have the protection of a supportive employer." Seth's hand brushes his arm, like a careful overture toward comfort. "Don't think of it as special treatment. Think of it as an investment we'd like to make."

When Seth puts it that way, some of the butterflies in Kieran's gut go away. But not all. He doesn't know if he's flattered or mortified. "You wouldn't make it if it weren't for me."

Seth huffs. "That's our fault."

Our fault. It weirds him out how Seth takes responsibility for all this shit, like it was his call. How he shoulders the blame for things he didn't do. "Yeah, well... don't beat yourself up about it."

"I'm not. I'm asking for your permission to schedule a safe-spaces training."

Kieran freezes, rubbing the back of his neck. "Oh. Uh. Go ahead. Do I have to be there?"

"No. Of course not."

"Thanks."

"If you think of anything else we could

do—anything at all that would make the office a place you'd be happy to be—tell me." Seth pauses, glancing around as they walk. "Where are we going?"

"Classy bar." Kieran's glad he changed the subject, because his cheeks are burning in the cold night air. He can't shake the feeling of being a nuisance; he's miserably embarrassed and excited by the thought of Seth doing this for him. But he can't argue, either. "Figured you'd want something upscale."

"I assumed you were taking me to—what was that gay bar?"

"Aiden's? Nah. Didn't want to scare you. Why, do you wanna?"

"No, thank you."

Kieran grins. He leads the way to the place he picked out, a fancy downtown cocktail lounge overlooking the river that runs through the middle of the city. It's the kind of place he'd never go himself, a swank and expensive joint, but with Seth, he thinks he can make an exception. Even if it means he'll only be able to afford one drink.

"This looks nice," Seth says, offensively surprised.

"Hey, I told you it was!"

"Well, it's *very* nice."

Kieran elbows him. "You fucking bet it is."

They get a booth by a window; the lounge has serious mood lighting, soft purples and blues and candles stacked at the end of the table. Outside, the river is lit up bright, bands of roving locals and tourists mingling on the River Walk. The waitress checks both their IDs—Seth looks surprised and flattered when she asks for his—and goes away with their drink orders. A frozen strawberry margarita for Kieran, and a scotch on the rocks for Seth, because apparently their alcoholic drink choices are the opposite of their Starbucks orders.

"See, man?" Kieran says. "You're young enough to look like a college freshman trying to drink at a bar."

"Fair enough," Seth says. The purple-blue lighting makes him look younger. Smiling does, too. "Would you like something to eat?"

"Oh, uh..." Kieran glances at the appetizer menu and wants to cry. Who the hell spends fifteen bucks on "gourmet fries"? "That's okay. They're pretty pricey."

Seth shrugs. Probably because he makes more

than seven bucks an hour at his job. "I don't mind," he says, and before Kieran can argue he's flagged down a waiter. "What do you want? I'll pay."

Kieran cannot deal with Seth buying him dinner on top of everything else he's done today. "You don't have to. It's fine."

Seth frowns. "Call me old, but it's better to eat something with alcohol. You have a young liver, but I don't. What do you want?"

Kieran chews on his lip, face red. "Uh, the fries. I guess."

Seth orders the fries and a plate of tiny, egregiously expensive crab sliders. Kieran tries to remember that the money doesn't mean anything to Seth, that he doesn't need to feel so mortified by the guy buying him dinner.

Then his margarita arrives, and it's huge. Big, red, and juicy, with a ripe strawberry on top. Kieran whoops, forgetting his mortification. "Don't know why you ordered scotch," he says, sucking the strawberry between his lips. "Fruity drinks, man."

Seth clears his throat and looks away. "I get enough sugar in my coffee."

"No, really?"

Seth smiles a little, and the conversation lapses, but Kieran can't let that happen, because he'll have to think about all the nice shit Seth keeps doing for him and then he'll feel weird. "Hey," he says, in desperation. "Tell me something about you."

"Like what?"

"Like anything. Tell me about Seth: the guy, not Seth: works for the Heidi Norton campaign. I feel like all I know about you is that you have a cat and spend way too much time staring at Marcus's guns. I'll say this for the guy—at least he works out."

Seth pretends not to hear that last part. "Well, you and I have the same degree."

"Where'd you get yours from?"

"UC Berkeley."

"How was California?"

"I liked it," Seth says. He looks out the window at the tourists wandering by. "It was hard to find a job I wanted. I had friends in San Antonio, so when I found work here, I came to join them. They all wound up moving away eventually. I'd been following Heidi Norton for a while, and I liked her campaign, so when I had the opportunity..."

"Wait, wait, wait." Kieran takes a bold swig of margarita and leans forward, elbows on the table. "I didn't dive into your life story just to wind up back at the campaign office. What'd you do before? Hell, what do you do now?"

"Apparently I go drinking with the office intern," Seth mutters, looking out the window.

"Yo, you go drinking with the only other queer—uh, sorry—nonheterosexual dude in the office. Not with *the intern*. Unless you're into interns." As usual, words come out of his mouth and the words are stupid. "I mean, into drinking with interns. Which is not cool. Drinking with interns on principle, I mean, is not cool. But drinking with *me*, that's very cool."

Seth's face goes through several emotional shifts, from bewildered to concerned to vaguely amused. "I suppose?"

"Yep." The food shows up then, thankfully, and Kieran gets to cramming fifteen dollars' worth of fries into his mouth. "Way to avoid the question," he adds, through a mouthful of potato.

"What do you do? Marathon soap operas? Laser tag?"

"History," Seth says. "I go to a lot of museums, and I read. Occasionally I marathon documentaries, if that counts as a marathon."

"So you spend a lot of time at home with a TV. Knew it."

Seth frowns. "Well..."

"Me, too. Except I don't have a cat. It'd be nicer if I did."

"I can introduce you to Dragon," Seth says, relaxing.

"Yeah?" Kieran's heart jumps, and for a moment he doesn't know why. Then he pictures going over to Seth's place, invading whatever squeaky-clean little bachelor pad he lives in, and snuggling Seth's cat, and... what?

Then he realizes. In his ideal world, this ends with *going back to Seth's place.* He's so fucked.

"These fries are great," he says. "Thanks."

"You're welcome." Seth is doing the thing again where he nibbles around the edges of his food, like he's waiting for them to get to a certain point before he digs in. "Thank you for staying late."

"Whatever. Not like you deserve to face a late-night campaign apocalypse alone." Kieran knocks back the rest of his margarita, which is objectively the best-tasting thing he's ever had. Even if it is fucking expensive. But hey, if Seth's buying the fries, the drink prices aren't so bad. "Wow. I'm so getting another one of those. Sure you don't wanna graduate from scotch?"

Seth swirls his boring-ass grown-up drink around in his glass and has a dignified sip. "No, thank you."

"Loser." Kieran waves the waiter over and orders another margarita, licking his lips—strawberry-tasting and sticky. He's warm, from his throat all the way to the pit of his stomach.

"All right," Seth says. "Tell me something about *you*."

"Huh?" Kieran coughs. "Uh, you kind of know everything."

"Do I?"

"Everything important."

"I don't know what you do outside of work."

Kieran groans. "I told you. TV. Alone. Sometimes my best friend invites herself over to make sure I'm alive. Occasional clubbing. If you really want to know something new, I've been told I get off on Facebook arguments."

Seth smiles like he isn't being told that Kieran is lonely and pathetic. "What are you watching these days?"

"I went through this whole phase where I wanted to watch every gay movie. I didn't realize I was queer till college, so I had a lot of time to make up. But that got old, so now I—" Kieran cringes. "Watch a lot of cartoons? I know, I could stand to get out more. I dunno, since I graduated I've been so busy trying to pay rent that I haven't exactly figured out the rest of *having a life*."

"You'll get there," Seth says. At least one of them sounds confident. "I didn't realize I was interested in men until I was older than you are, if that makes you feel any better."

Seth being attracted to dudes is not a safe subject for Kieran's brain, so as usual, he tries to make it into a joke. "Was it the first time Marcus showed up in a tank top?"

Seth does the thing where he smiles while trying to look reproving. "No. It was a bit before that."

"Have you... dated a lot?" Kieran can see Seth's

face crumple slightly, as if he expects Kieran to judge him for the wrong answer. He adds hastily, "I'm just asking because I haven't. I mean, I feel like I missed out on a lot of opportunities by not coming out until later. I didn't know what was going on with me, so I didn't want to be with anyone. I had this whole ice-queen persona."

"You don't say," Seth says. He smiles again, the tension easing from his face. "I didn't have much time to date men. There were a few, but then I met Marian, and that consumed a few years, and since then I haven't... wanted to bother."

"Did she have a problem with you being bi?" Kieran bites his lip as it occurs to him that the question might be a painful one. "I mean, if that's a question you wanna answer. Sorry."

Seth shakes his head, looks away. "No. She didn't particularly care about that. It would be nice if it were that simple, I think." He pauses, presses the tips of his fingers to his lips. "She and I didn't communicate well. We didn't make each other happy. That's all."

He glances at Kieran and then clears his throat, picking up his knife and fork. He looks downcast, even though he does a decent job of covering it up, and Kieran kicks himself. The last thing he wants to do is make Seth *sad* after today.

Kieran rubs his face. "Well, you make me happy."

It comes out too soft, too genuine, too different from his usual sarcasm and bite. It makes Seth look up, an expression on his face that Kieran can't read—confusion? Hope? Honest surprise that Kieran said something nice? The corners of his eyes crinkle up as he stares at Kieran, and more words trip out of Kieran's mouth. "I mean, I think you have a lot of good qualities. This whole thing with the safe spaces training... I really appreciate it. Maybe someone else would've done it, but not in a way that made me feel *okay*, you know? So what-ever you had going on with Marian, I think your communication skills are fine."

For me.

Seth blinks slowly, and Kieran cringes at him-self. He just completely panicked because Seth looked sad. Seth probably really, really didn't need a motivational speech.

A second later, though, it's all worth it because Seth's eyes soften and he smiles. "I'm glad," he says.

* * *

The longer they sit and talk, the more Kieran realizes he's bound to embarrass himself where Seth is concerned. He has a growing, horrifying suspicion that it's obvious how everything Seth does is endearing to him.

Everything Seth does—like eating fries and sliders with impeccable table manners—makes Kieran want to stay there all night, even for the awkward parts. He wants to know more. Wants to crack Seth open and memorize him.

"So... you're a history nut. What kinda history?"

Seth coughs. "Well, ordinarily I'd say 'the history of political movements.'"

"Ordinarily?"

"Since it's you—I study gay history. The social movements, and so forth." Seth carefully cuts a wedge out of his last slider with a knife and fork. "I like to stay connected with the—with *our* history."

"But you don't go out and dance? Ever? Not even to study the rich history of gay bars?"

Seth shakes his head.

Kieran purses his lips and takes a gulp of his second margarita. "Maybe you should. Y'know, lots of guys could be lured in by the promise of a good-looking single man with a cat."

Seth waves a hand as if to silence him, and it's hard to tell in the colorful lounge lights, but his face looks hot. Like, warm.

Also the other kind of hot.

"I'm just saying," Kieran says. "You'd have better luck at a bar than you're gonna have with Mr. Straight-and-Disorganized."

"I know," Seth says. He punctuates it by draining the rest of his scotch. When the waiter circles back again, he orders a glass of water for each of them. "I'll have you know I'm not holding out any hope that Marcus will suddenly abandon his fiancée and child and—"

He doesn't seem capable of finishing the sentence, so Kieran gives it a shot. "Make you his new Mrs. Norton?"

Seth scowls at him. "Yes, thank you. I would never want him to. He's happy as he is, and I have a great deal of respect for his fiancée. I have no hope of getting anything from him."

"So let him go! Go moon over other guys.

Cuter guys. Smarter, less heterosexual, more single guys. More organized guys. Or gals."

Seth pinches the bridge of his nose and stares down at the table. "I don't know if that would help."

"Come on, why not? You already dress sharp—all you need to do is loosen that tie, go swagger into a club somewhere, and take your pick of the nice, interesting people in there."

"Is that how it works, in your experience?"

Kieran huffs and flips his hair over his shoulder. "Obviously. Do I look like a guy who doesn't get what he wants?"

Seth sighs. He reaches up and loosens his tie a fraction. "Well, maybe it isn't an issue for you."

"Are you kidding? I'm trans. If *I* can go out, you can go out."

"I—" As expected, Seth can't argue with that. He frowns instead, and finally eats his sliders.

Kieran triumphantly drains his margarita. It's like swallowing a mouthful of candy. "Oh my God, I could drink ten of these. Except I'd go broke."

"Do you have work in the morning?"

"At my shitty day job," Kieran says, scrunching up his face. "Don't remind me."

Seth smiles. "As your supervisor, I think I should recommend that you stop drinking."

"I'm not a *huge* lightweight." Never mind that he feels floaty and content in a decidedly unsober way. On second thought, maybe Seth has a point. "But uh, I guess. To be responsible." He does want Seth to think he's responsible. In a weird way, he's always wanted Seth to think he's good at what he does.

Seth checks his watch. "It's getting late."

"Yeah, yeah. Lemme stuff these fries in and you can get home to your damn cat."

"I don't mean to rush you. Take your time, and I'll take you home."

Kieran blinks. "You don't have to. The bus runs late."

Seth gives him a pointed look. "I'd feel better if I gave you a ride."

Which, all right, it'd be better than huddling at the bus stop, half-drunk in the dark and hoping this isn't the day that some weird asshole decides to mess with him. "Thanks."

Seth nods, sipping at his water. The waiter comes; Seth gives them his card.

Kieran gazes after their server. "Hey, uh—what about my check?"

Seth shrugs. "Don't worry about it. If we were paying you, you'd have worked overtime tonight." He smiles. "Consider this your payment."

The margaritas alone definitely cost more than he'd have earned in an hour or two, but Kieran doesn't argue, because he's not sure what'll come out of his mouth if he opens it. The words in his mouth are all *I'm usually a cheaper date than this*, and he's not, *not* gonna say that out loud.

Instead he winds up mumbling, "Thank you."

Seth makes another dismissive noise. He signs the check, tips their server, and offers Kieran a hand out of the booth. It's all Kieran can do to wipe the potato grease off his fingers before he grabs Seth's hand. The room is definitely on the unsteady side, and he's maybe more than half-drunk. Still, when he focuses hard, he manages to walk after Seth in a straight line.

Outside, it's a nice temperature—cool, but still mild from the heat of the day. Seth takes him by the shoulder gently to steer him toward the inside of the sidewalk, away from the street, and keeps himself between Kieran and the occasional cars that roll by. Kieran rubs his shoulder. He could deal with being drunk and having Seth steer him around more often.

"Why're you being so nice to me?" he asks, half-laughing, half-serious. "What's in it for you?"

Seth smiles. "To be honest, I'm glad you came along."

"Tired of being the only one?"

"You could say that. It's almost a relief that someone finally noticed how I—" Seth squares his shoulders, looking away peevishly. "How I feel about Marcus."

"You mean your big bisexual crush on him."

"If you have to call it that."

"You're glad?"

"I forgot what it was like to be around people who notice." Seth makes a strangled noise that might be a laugh. "And I appreciate your bluntness. Otherwise I never would have known I wasn't alone."

Kieran finds himself grinning, rubbing his face in an effort to wipe off the blush. "That's a first."

They get to Seth's car, and Seth shepherds him briskly into the passenger seat. Kieran curls up and listens, barely following but interested, as Seth tells him about the early origins of the gay liberation movement and occasionally asks for clarification on the GPS directions to Kieran's apartment.

They arrive at Kieran's apartment all too soon. Seth, of course, nice dude that he is, gets out of the car to see Kieran up to his door—only he stops Kieran, catching his sleeve as he starts to turn away from the car. "Just a minute," he says. "About the office. There's—something I wanted to ask you."

"Ugh." Kieran makes a face. The office makes him think of *safe-spaces training* and *Seth being nice* and he doesn't want to contemplate either when he's this tipsy.

Seth frowns, clasping his hands behind his back. "I had a word with Marcus. This office is expected to grow as the campaign carries on, and we could use a larger full-time staff. I understand you'd need to quit your restaurant job, so don't feel like you have to rush to a decision, but—" Seth pauses when Kieran reels back and stares at him. "If there were a position available, would you take it?"

"Are you kidding?" Kieran wheezes. He doesn't know what his chest is doing, but he can barely breathe. "Are you serious? *Full-time?*"

"I told Marcus that your work ethic already makes you invaluable, and he agreed. If we have the funding—and I believe we will—we'd like to hire you properly. Real paychecks and everything." Seth smiles tentatively. "If you're interested, that is. After our conversation the other day, I wasn't sure if this was what you wanted."

There are either hearts or dollar signs dancing in Kieran's eyes, or maybe both. "I—*yes*. Of course I'm interested!"

Seth's anxious smile relaxes into something relieved. "Good. I'll let Marcus know."

"Thank you. Thank you, thank you, I mean it." Kieran can't believe Seth is shaking his head, like he expects Kieran to let him brush this off too. "Seth, this is nuts. I can't—"

"You deserve it." Seth clears his throat. "You don't need to thank me. But for the time being, you have work in the morning, so you should go in."

"Okay. Sure. But I'm *gonna* thank you." Kieran lets Seth take his arm and help him up the stairs, because he does feel like he might fall over otherwise. "Holy shit."

"Remember to drink enough water."

"Yeah, yeah, I will. You know—" Kieran ducks his head, because his face is all red and they're about to walk under the light of his porch lamp. "When I showed up on that first day, I thought you were an asshole," he mumbles. "Like, stick-up-your-ass and everyone was scared of you."

Seth's face pinches up. "Well. I'm sorry."

"No, that's the point. I was wrong. Even though I'm always right." Kieran slumps up the last stair to his apartment door, Seth trailing after him, and fumbles through his satchel to find his keys. "You're great. You're so great. That's why I keep saying you should go clubbing. You should have fun. Be happy. You deserve to be happy. I don't think you're an asshole at all, just, like—just a guy who doesn't have enough fun."

In the weak glow of the lamp above Kieran's door, Seth smiles, but he looks tired. Lonely. "Thank you."

"Thanks?"

"For the recommendation." His lips twitch. "And for the categorization of my faults. I appreciate it."

"No, no, *no*. That's not what I mean." Kieran forgets about his keys. Instead he grabs for the banister next to where Seth's hand is gripping and winds up gripping his hand instead, Seth's skin startlingly hot under his fingers. "I meant what I said earlier. You *deserve* better. Like, way better. Like m—" Words. Fucking falling out of his mouth. But now he's said them, so he might as well keep going. "Like me. For instance. For example. If you'd rather not hit up the club. I'm just saying there are guys who would date you. Like me."

Seth blinks, and for a moment his nice, mean, glinty eyes are wide and startled. Then he starts to back away, hand slipping out from under Kieran's fingers. "Go to bed, Kieran. I'll see you at w—"

Kieran grabs his tie by the knot and reels him back in. The warm flush of the margarita seems to be rolling through his head now, and when his knuckles brush against Seth's skin past the one un-done button of his shirt, his pulse jumps. "I'm se-rious right now."

"You're drunk right now," Seth says sharply.

"Doesn't make a difference," Kieran retorts, and kisses him. He has to lurch up on his toes to kiss him, and he's wobbly, so he grabs the rail for balance and pulls Seth against him by the tie.

Wow, he could get used to Seth's disapproving little mouth in this context. His lips are really soft—

Then Seth isn't kissing him anymore, he's pulling Kieran's satchel from his shoulder and locating Kieran's keys and jamming them into the door with more force than necessary.

Kieran leans dizzily against the banister, a sinking feeling in his gut. "Hey. Seth."

"Good night," Seth says, holding the door open, Kieran's keys and satchel in his other hand.

Kieran opens his mouth, and for once, nothing comes out. He takes his stuff and slinks inside, past Seth, flattening his body against the door so he doesn't have to touch him.

Door closes. Kieran sits on the floor. Listens to Seth's shoes scrambling down the stairs, and the car's engine starting. He hugs his satchel to his chest and listens to Seth drive away.

He feels sick, and it's not from the booze.

6.

Kieran is spared the total indignity of returning to the office for three whole days. Which, instead of savoring, he spends being furious and sullen at his shitty restaurant job, marathoning the dumbest cooking shows he can find, and getting irrationally angry every time Jillian posts a cute selfie with her new girlfriend.

Speaking of Jillian, after he fails to reply to any of her demands for details about his "hot date" with Seth, she gets the hint and just comes over with booze and hugs. She doesn't make him talk about it. She's good like that.

Rejected by his *supervisor*. His supervisor who barely liked him, anyway, who he decided to kiss for no fucking good reason, who offered Kieran the opportunity of his life, who probably wants nothing to do with him now.

Kieran's not sure if he feels more humiliated or stupid or—maybe just sad. He's not sure how to deal with feeling sad. Sure, he deals with a lot of bullshit in his life, the kind that should make him weepy on a regular basis. Mostly he gets by, by feeling annoyed and superior and like he'd rather drink alone than suffer the company of fools.

His expectations are usually so low that he's not used to feeling disappointed. But for half a second, they'd been so high.

The night before he has to go back to work at the office, he almost convinces himself to quit—to totally commit to never seeing Seth again, sparing himself the uncomfortable silence. He'd be doing Seth a favor; Seth must regret that job offer now, must be trying to think of a way to retract it. Well, it wasn't official anyway.

Kieran can't quite bring himself to pick up the phone—he's not *quite* that dramatic—so instead he lies facedown on his bed for hours and wishes he at least had a cat.

When he gets tired of suffocating in a pillow, he goes back to his other major form of recreation:

scrolling through Facebook and glaring at his happy friends. Halfway down his feed, though, Aiden's has an ad. "Go-Go Boys Night Out at Aiden's... Saturday Only, No Cover!"

Kieran chews on his lip and stares at the attached photo: a burly dude in a thong posing under bright pink lights.

It's an idea. What if, instead of quitting, he strolled into the campaign office tomorrow with a mild, sexy hangover and a bunch of hickeys? Whoever said the cure for loneliness wasn't grinding on a bunch of cute guys?

Before he can talk himself out of it, he's rolled out of bed and into his clubbing eyeliner. He doesn't text Jillian, because she'd worry. He pulls his hair back in a loose ponytail, leaving a few sultry curls hanging down the side of his face, and puts on the most revealing tank he has that doesn't show his binder. He admires himself in the mirror for a while, then stuffs the pockets of his skinny jeans with his ID, cash for drinks, and—on second thought—a condom or two.

* * *

Aiden's is a cute little shack, an unkempt bar with a rainbow flag hanging over the door, windows plastered with flyers advertising the nightly drink and dance specials. The first floor is the bar proper, and usually quiet, with older and shyer patrons hanging around and sipping their drinks. But the floor hums underfoot: down a flight of practically medieval stone stairs is the basement dance club.

Since there's no line, Kieran snags a piña colada from the bar before he makes his way downstairs. He brushes past a couple of tall, pretty girls he recognizes from another night at Aiden's. The basement dance floor is hot and loud and dark, pink disco ball spinning above the floor, strobe chopping up the moments between pulses of light. There's a good-sized crowd dancing, and a cluster of people around the bar against the far wall. The DJ is playing some questionable dubstep, and Kieran works his way around the edge of the dance floor, planning to lounge attractively near the alcohol until the music improves.

As he gets closer to the bar, he notices an obstruction in the midst of the tipsy club-goers trying to get their drinks. Someone square-shouldered and out of place, flattened against the bar but not ordering.

He knows it's Seth by the body language alone. By the shirt and tie, so intimidatingly crisp in the office, so stiff and weird in the club. By the neat Boy Scout hair, staying stubbornly in place despite the heat and the people jostling around him. Still, Kieran doesn't want to think it's actually him, so he keeps wandering closer, dubstep pumping in his ears like a second heartbeat, waiting for the image to resolve itself into someone else, some total stranger.

By the time he's close enough to admit the truth, Seth sees him, too. Kieran's one consolation is that Seth looks as horrified to see him as Kieran feels.

Kieran thinks about turning his back and walking right out of Aiden's. He could make a dramatic exit, flip his hair and stalk off into the night, and no one would even have to know that he was going back to a lonely, shitty, empty apartment to watch TV dramas with a sad assortment of stuffed animals.

But his drink is still ice cold in his hand, and this is *his* fucking club.

Instead he stalks up and grabs Seth by the sleeve, yanking him forward. "Don't stand at the bar if you're not gonna order, jackass," he snips, not caring if Seth can hear him over the music. Seth, wide-eyed, lets Kieran tow him off to the hallway that leads to the bathrooms, which is about the only place not packed with dancers and relatively quiet.

Once they're alone, Kieran drops Seth's sleeve, disgusted. "What are you *doing* in here?"

Seth stares at him, prim and lost. "I'm sorry. I didn't think you'd be here."

Ugly disappointment settles in the pit of Kieran's stomach. "Wow, so you show up at the club *I* told you about? Nice plan, asshole."

"Kieran, I..." Seth breaks off with a huff of nervous breath, running his fingers through his neat hair, roughing it up. "I should apologize for—for a few nights ago."

"Are you fucking kidding? No. You don't need to apologize for *that*. You're not into me, I get it. Whatever. Plenty of guys don't like me. I feel pretty stupid about kissing you, honestly. But what you *don't* do is barge into my favorite club, looking for—" He can't imagine. "What *are* you doing here?"

Seth looks so miserable. He presses his back up against the wall, glancing down at the floor as a few dancers shuffle past them toward the bathrooms. "Finding a distraction."

"A distraction from *what*?" Suddenly Kieran remembers his own damn advice. "Oh. Finally going to find a guy to tear you away from Marcus?"

"No," Seth says. "From you."

Kieran blinks. He frowns up at Seth's face for a minute while Seth stares at the wall, his shoulders hunched.

He steps back, leaving Seth to lean against the opposite wall while he takes a steadying slurp of his piña colada.

"Are you saying you *like* me?"

"Yes," Seth says, and he swallows, and then— "I'm aware that it's—it's inappropriate, and as your supervisor I shouldn't feel this way, and as your *supervisor*, I don't. I respect you very much. And as a person, as a man who made me think about the possibility of being with someone again..."

"You like me?"

Seth breathes out. With his hair askew, he looks torn down. "Yes. I'm sorry. I never meant for you to find out. I was hoping to find someone—"

"Hey!" Kieran doesn't know if he's feeling more elation or outrage, but luckily, he has the lung capacity for both. "Go back to the part where you like me and explain why you ran off like a punk bitch when I kissed you."

Seth is almost definitely blushing, and mortified, and staring at the ceiling. Staring anywhere but at Kieran. "You were drunk."

"Oh, yeah? Well, I'm sober now."

"I'm *old*," Seth mumbles. "I'm an old man who can't hold down a relationship."

"Not with *that* attitude. When was the last time you tried?"

Seth looks at him. Sort of sideways, but it's a start. Is this what it's like to be Marcus? Going through life every day with Seth totally unable to look him in the eye?

Nope—because Marcus has no idea what he's missing out on. "Look, jerk. I'm kinda into you, too. And we're here." Kieran crosses the hall to him, grabs one of his hands, and presses against his chest. "If you're young enough to show up at a club and dance, you're young enough to try dating me. Okay? That's my rule."

Seth hesitates. "Is it?"

"I made it up. For you." Kieran tosses back the rest of his drink and pitches his empty plastic cup in the direction of the nearest trash can. "And I chugged my piña colada for you. So—let's dance."

"I really don't know how to dance," Seth says softly, letting Kieran draw in closer to hear him.

Kieran grins. "Fuck, you think I do?"

He leans up and kisses Seth again. For the first time, maybe, because this is the first time Seth has let Kieran coax him into kissing back, following when Kieran tugs gently at his lip. One of Seth's hands lands on his waist. Light, careful.

Kieran reaches up and undoes the top button of Seth's shirt, bumps his nose against Seth's, and asks, "Dance with me?"

Seth's fingers curl, just so, into the hem of Kieran's shirt. "All right."

Kieran grabs him by the hand and pulls him out of the hallway and onto the floor, where the heat of the crowd rolls over him as he presses back into the cluster of dancers. Seth follows, but he's only watching Kieran. Not the crowd. Not the lights. He doesn't even seem to mind that the DJ's still playing terrible dubstep—deep, shuddery bass that Kieran feels in his toes when he leans up to wrap his arms around Seth's shoulders and pull him in.

It's awkward. It's a bit weird to be kissing in the middle of the crowd, bumped and jostled by passing dancers. He feels like he's grinning too much, too happy to feel Seth wrap his arms around the dip of Kieran's back and hold him close.

A song with a decent beat comes on and Kieran wriggles loose, throwing his hands in the air and dancing like a fucking idiot. Seth gapes at him like a fish out of water, and Kieran grabs him by the tie, dragging him into a nice deep kiss and rubbing up against his chest, feeling Seth's startled little gasp when Kieran's packer rubs against his junk. Then Seth's palm is squeezing his ass, and they're back to half-dancing, half-grinding, and Seth is laughing helplessly against his mouth.

Kieran's drenched in sweat by the end of the fifth song—binding and clubbing is *never* a good combo—and Seth, overdressed as he is, doesn't look much better. His hair is a mess, all scrambled up by Kieran's hands having combed through it, and his mouth is flushed under the lights. A disco ball overhead sends silver spots glittering across his throat, and Kieran leans up to follow them with his mouth, pressing kisses all the way up to Seth's ear and nuzzling against his one tiny earring. The next song is Britney Spears, so Kieran summons the last of his dancing energy, working his body against Seth's and feeling Seth's hands map out the curve of his back.

When the track ends, he makes a gesture toward the stairs, and Seth nods, squeezing his hand as they work their way out of the crowd.

Upstairs is freezing by comparison to the dance floor, a merciful chill that has Kieran shivering and leaning on Seth's shoulder as they stumble through the quiet bar and out the door to the street. His ears are ringing, still thrumming along to the bass they left behind.

"Not bad for a first-timer," Kieran says.

Seth is pink under the streetlights. "That was—it was fun."

"Yeah? Think you could stand to go again sometime?"

"I could certainly try," Seth says, with a smile.

Kieran goes up on his toes for another kiss, and

this time Seth leans down, catching his mouth and gently winding an arm around Kieran's back. Once Kieran is kissing him, he doesn't want to stop, never mind how smart it isn't to make out in the street at night. The cold air starts to seep into his clothes, which is one more reason to press closer, curling his shivering fingers into the collar of Seth's shirt.

He definitely notices when Seth gets hard. Of course, that's apparently another thing that Seth is bound to feel bad about, because he abruptly extracts himself from Kieran's arms and starts to back off. "I—"

"It's cool," Kieran says. "If my dick could stand up on its own, it would've by now."

Seth stares at him, adorably off-balance. He relaxes a little when Kieran reaches out and grabs his hand, squeezing it, but he still doesn't seem to know what to say.

"Just to be clear," Kieran says. "I'm up for whatever's in your comfort zone. Like, for example, sex."

Seth clears his throat, his thumb running over Kieran's knuckles in nervous circles. "I-I want you to know that this won't impact your employment opportunities. In any way."

Kieran leans in close. "I didn't think it would."

Seth swallows. "My car isn't very far. If you'd like to come over, maybe have a drink—"

Kieran grins.

* * *

Seth's car is nice. Kieran was too tipsy to appreciate it before, but now he does, splaying in the passenger seat while Seth—face pink, lips red—starts the car, his eyes fixed on the road.

"How long've you liked me?" Kieran asks.

Seth's throat works nervously. "Oh, I don't know."

"Totally unromantic. Try again."

"I didn't realize until you told me you knew I was interested in Marcus."

"Wow. Well, with the crush you had going for him, I guess I don't blame you for not realizing early on how irresistible I am." Kieran grins when Seth shoots a look at him. "I always thought you were hot. It was just a matter of realizing that you were also, y'know, kind of... great."

Seth doesn't quite seem to buy the assessment

of himself as *hot and great*. "I'm glad you think so," he mutters. Kieran is fully prepared to repeat himself, but holds back because Seth looks like he's working himself up to something. He drives for a minute in tense silence, and then abruptly starts: "Look, Kieran—are you really all right with this? I won't be angry if you'd rather not even think about a relationship with me. I'm twelve years older than you, and believe it or not, I try *not* to date my coworkers, let alone—"

"Whatever," Kieran interjects.

Seth scowls incredulously at him.

"I like you. You *are* hot and great. The least we can do is try this out." He leans over and bumps his shoulder against Seth's. "And I don't give a shit about you being old and weird. Obviously."

"Thank you, I think." Seth is still frowning, still wrestling with himself. "I don't want you to feel any pressure—"

"I don't. I believe you, okay? I know you'd let it go if I wasn't interested, but I am." Kieran actually, for once in his life, tries to sound serious, because he wants the tension in Seth's face to ease.

Seth lets out a tight breath, looking around Kieran when they pause at a stoplight. "As long as you know that I respect you, and care about you—regardless—and that I want what's best for you."

"Okay," Kieran says. "You're the best thing that's happened to me in ages."

Seth blinks several times, and then looks back at the road hastily as if snapping out of a dream, blushing to his ears. He doesn't say anything, but the expression on his face is trembling somewhere between bafflement and happiness, and Kieran can work with that.

They pull up at Seth's place a few minutes of comfortable silence later. Seth's apartment is, of course, nice; it's in a bland neighborhood, but Kieran's not surprised. Not by the interior, either: a neat, sparse little one-bedroom with a TV and a couch and not a lot else. It's all pinned up and tidy, just like Seth.

Except for the glowering lump of black fur huddled on top of the sofa when they come in. "Hi, Dragon," Seth says, in a tone of voice Kieran has never heard him use, not even with Marcus's baby. He leaves Kieran's side to pet the lump, which makes a squeaky meow and begins to purr.

"She's cute," Kieran says, with trepidation.

Cats don't always like him, but Dragon lets him scratch her under her chin and behind her fluffy tufted ears, while Seth gets two glasses and pours wine for both of them. Kieran's starting to feel gross, sweaty and clubbed-out, but then again Seth's in the same boat—unkempt, and smelling like the combined sweat of a hundred tipsy dancers. Kieran cozies onto the couch with him anyway. "Where were we?"

Seth blushes and takes a steadying sip of wine. "I think—I think I was in the middle of leading up to the Stonewall Riots."

Kieran snorts. "Oh yeah? Did you live through those?"

"That was *nineteen sixty-nine*."

"Wow, not so old now, old man."

Seth huffs, and launches into the epic tale of midcentury queer politics. Kieran gets comfy—because he is interested, in spite of himself, and because it's fun to watch Seth try to focus on history talk when Kieran is running his fingers along the inside of his thigh. As soon as they're done drinking the wine, he grabs Seth's hand, cutting him off mid-rant. "Hey. You're disgusting."

Seth blinks.

"And I'm disgusting, too. So what say you show me around your shower?"

"Oh," Seth says, blank. Then he seems to recover, and smiles, almost shyly. "All right."

* * *

"Do you need any pointers?" Kieran drawls, sitting on the bathroom counter. "Or a pep talk?"

Seth gives him a strange look, loosening his tie. His fingers work elegantly into the folds of the knot, already slightly askew from Kieran yanking on it. "Why do you ask?"

"I dunno, you don't act like you've ever taken your clothes off in front of somebody else."

"I was *married*."

"I mean, I guess, but I don't like assuming what you did with your ex-wife." Kieran eyes him, up and down. "So. Have you?"

"It's funny you should ask." Seth folds his tie and leaves it next to the sink. Unbuttons his shirt with a nimble touch. "This is usually the part of relationships I'm good at." His mouth quirks up when he says it, but it's not quite a smile.

Kieran doesn't know what to do with that look, other than pull his own shirt over his head and look inviting. Fortunately, Seth takes the bait. He comes in close and smooths his hands along Kieran's sides, making no distinction between the binder and his skin. His hands stop at Kieran's hips, and he hesitates. "Is there anything I should know," he begins, "about what you—how you prefer to be touched, or called, or anything like that?"

Kieran shrugs, pleased. "I'm not big on 'girly-bits' or 'ladyparts,'" he says. "Other than that, whatever. I like my body."

Seth smiles a little. "I do too."

There's still a part of Kieran that bristles with nerves as he unbuttons his jeans and kicks them down, but Seth's watching him with careful intensity, with a restrained admiration that makes Kieran's skin prickle with appreciation. He wriggles out of his binder and leans back on the sink, letting Seth look at him as he reaches down and squeezes his packer through his underwear.

Seth swallows.

"How are you with, uh—?" Kieran has said this to guys before, is not a blushing virgin, but his face starts to turn red anyway. *Spit it out. The worst he can do is freak out.* "How are you with bottom-ing?"

Seth sucks in a breath. "I—I prefer it. Actually."

"Cool. Because I sort of, uh, prepared for that situation, if you wanna."

"It's—it has been a while. I'm not sure I have any condoms. Do we need one?"

"Safety first." Kieran ducks down and squirrels his condom and lube packet out of his jeans. "Got you covered. You were gonna go find a guy in a club and you didn't bring condoms?"

Seth takes them delicately. "I didn't really think it through. I suppose I would've had to buy some. You're... much more prepared for this than I am."

"I kinda hoped I'd find someone to mess around with tonight." Kieran straightens up, hooking his fingers through Seth's belt loops and tugging gently. "Trying to take my mind off, y'know, you. I guess I dodged that bullet." He has to smile at the flash of startled, soft emotion that jumps into Seth's eyes. "Hey, are you gonna take your pants off any time soon?"

Seth blinks. "Yes. Sorry."

He unbuttons his pants and lets Kieran pull them down. His legs have a certain gangly charm, but Kieran is honestly more interested in his dick, pressing hard against the front of his underwear.

Kieran tugs his briefs down, glancing up at Seth as he wraps a hand around Seth's cock, letting its weight settle in his hand. Seth makes a strangled noise.

"Nice," Kieran says.

"Thank you," Seth says, stiffly. "Will you—in a minute I'm going to be too embarrassed to do anything. Can we get in the shower?"

"No problem, boss."

"Thank you, *coffee boy*."

Kieran laughs and shoves off his own underwear, absently gripping his own dick, the packer slung around his hips on the harness he bought specifically for those nights out at the club. Seth switches on the water, and Kieran scoots underneath the showerhead with him, the hot water cascading down his back and washing away the sweat of the club. Seth is breathing carefully, like he's doing his best not to appear overly excited, although his dick is communicating that on his behalf. He also can't seem to keep his eyes off Kieran, which is exactly what Kieran revels in.

"Deep breaths," Kieran reminds him. "I know. It's a lot to take in. I'm pretty hot."

Seth makes a sour lemon face. "I'll try my best to handle it."

"Let me know if I'm going too fast on you. Don't wanna blow your mind too hard."

"As I said," Seth grumbles, "this is the part I'm *relatively* comfortable with."

Kieran grins, reaching up and tangling his fingers in Seth's hair. "Then I'd hate to see you uncomfortable."

Seth mutters indignantly and kisses him, hands coming up to cradle the back of Kieran's head as he pushes Kieran against the wall of the shower, his cock brushing Kieran's thigh. Kieran reaches down and squeezes his dick, gently working it in his hand as Seth shudders and pushes his tongue into Kieran's mouth. The soft, muffled sounds Seth makes at the back of his throat while they're kissing are the hottest things Kieran's heard in a long time, and okay—for a guy who acts like his last relationship was several centuries ago, Seth is a pretty good kisser, eager and coaxing all at once.

Seth's half-smiling when he draws back, his hair spiky and punked out from Kieran's hands combing through it. "Can I—? Would you like it if I—" Seth pauses for a moment too long, and then the words jumble out of his mouth all at once. "If I sucked your cock, would it be—good? For you?"

"It'd be a good show," Kieran says, cracking a grin. "Go on, show me your skills."

"It's been a while," Seth mumbles. "I don't know what *skills* I have left."

He's remarkably eager to get on his knees, water dripping down his face as he settles between Kieran's legs and wraps a hand around his cock. Kieran's throat jumps, a jolt of arousal leaping through him at the sight of Seth, wet and rumpled, leaning in to slide his lips down Kieran's dick.

There's something unbearably sensual about the way he moves. It doesn't matter that he's sucking on silicone; he still looks like he's tasting it, like it's a part of Kieran he wants to explore and savor. He runs his tongue along the underside to the tip so Kieran can see, and Kieran can *feel* it, his cock pressing heavy on Seth's tongue.

Their eyes meet, and Kieran is frozen by the intensity of that sensation, barely able to breathe.

It feels so good he could almost cry.

"I—I guess it's like riding a bicycle." He's stammering. Shaky. "Haha. Hey. *Bi*cycle."

There's nothing quite like seeing a guy try to glare at you with a mouthful of silicone cock.

Kieran can't help laughing, slumping helplessly against the shower wall. Then Seth presses forward, his hand twisting around the base of Kieran's packer, pressing it against his clit—and Kieran hears himself groan, loud and sharp, his back going stiff against the wall. Okay, maybe Seth isn't the only one who hasn't gotten laid in a while. The gentle, grinding pressure gets Kieran's nerves on edge, and he ruts against it, nudging his cock deeper into Seth's mouth. Seth tightens his grip and pushes Kieran back against the wall; Kieran whines, running his nails along Seth's scalp.

The pressure's not enough, and not at the right angle to make him come—not quite—but it's enough to send a flush crawling up his chest, pleasure spiking through his abdomen. Seth's eyes are closed, eyelids fluttering as he mouths at Kieran's dick, and the need, the bliss in his face is suddenly too much for Kieran to handle.

"I gotta fuck you," Kieran gasps. "Seth, c'mon. Let's go."

Seth glances up at him, a slow look that makes Kieran's stomach churn with craving for him. He pulls off Kieran's cock with a final long suck, which he punctuates with a twist at the shaft that makes Kieran shiver all the way to his toes. "Bed?" he asks, hands on his knees, dick hard between his legs.

"Yeah. Bed."

Kieran barely dries off with the towel Seth tosses at him, squeezing the water out of his long hair but stumbling out of the bathroom with trails of water still rolling down his chest and legs. Seth's bedroom is sparse, clean, blue—that's all Kieran bothers to absorb before he's falling into the bed, straddling Seth's cock and running his hands down his chest. He grinds against Seth's stomach for the way the packer rubs his clit, riding it while Seth kisses him. Then Seth tips him over and crawls on top of him, hair dripping, and picks up the condom and lube.

Kieran gazes up at him, sweeping his eyes over Seth's long, skinny frame, the soft flecks of dark hair on his chest, his nipples hard and pink. His expression of intent concentration as he rolls the condom down on Kieran's packer and rips open the packet of lube. "Hey," Kieran says, "no rush—don't you need, like, prep?"

Seth pauses and looks abashed. "I, ah. No, I don't."

Kieran scoffs. "Are you sure? Because most guys do, and I'm not gonna hurt you."

"It's not that." Seth clears his throat. "I—I took care of that earlier, before... before I decided to go out."

"Wowww." Kieran can't choose between amused and turned on, and he hopes his tone conveys a little of both. He grabs Seth by the hips. "Okay. Then get your ass on my cock, boss."

"Please stop calling me that," Seth groans. He slicks up Kieran's cock and lowers himself onto it, nice and slow, with a careful hiss as he sinks down to take it in completely. The pressure takes Kieran's breath away for a moment, and he forces himself to stay still, to not chase after the sensation by rolling his hips up and fucking into Seth before he's settled.

Seth runs his hands down Kieran's chest slowly, bracing himself, breathing deeply. "Oh." He mutters, half to himself, "I forgot what this is like."

"You're so *hot*," Kieran moans. "I'm so fucking glad."

Seth wipes his hair out of his face with a shaky smile. "Glad?"

"That you're not screwing some other lucky guy at the club right now?" Kieran runs his hands down Seth's legs, liking the soft scrape of Seth's hair under his palms. "That you're into me?"

"I'm glad you came and found me." Seth bends down and kisses him, one of those deep kisses Kieran just wants to sink into, and then he starts to rock his hips, sliding up on Kieran's dick and taking him deep again. He moans into Kieran's mouth with the motion and bites his lip, enough to sting. His hands squeeze Kieran's chest, stroke his sides, and Kieran wraps his arms around Seth's back, pushing up, groaning when the base of the packer rubs all along his clit.

He's so *wet*, and so hungry for it—he almost yelps when Seth works himself deep on his cock, grinding into him, rutting him toward an orgasm that feels like months in the making.

Kieran reaches between them to palm Seth's dick, tugging it, matching the slow rolls of Seth's hips. Seth shudders and hangs his head, pressing his cheek to Kieran's shoulder, his stubble scraping at Kieran's collarbone. "Fuck," he whispers, barely a breath. His hips stutter, push back hard.

Kieran's not really interested in making this last; they've both been waiting a long time, and he wants to come, wants Seth to come with him. He grips Seth's cock and jerks him off, arching his hips up and grinding himself to completion, a white-hot burst of pleasure that makes his whole body squeeze tight, tight, tight—then feels Seth moan and come across his stomach, sticky and hot.

"Fuck," Kieran says. He deflates into the bed, head spinning.

Seth lets out a long sigh that seems to indicate agreement. He climbs gingerly off of Kieran's cock and collapses into the sheets at Kieran's side, his head landing on Kieran's shoulder.

Kieran sighs. "We gotta shower again."

"Mm."

Kieran turns his head, bumps his forehead against Seth's. "Can I, um... can I sleep here?"

"Of course." Seth draws a hesitant breath. "You're still interested in the job?"

"Of course I am. The only way I wasn't gonna say yes is if you changed your mind about wanting me there."

"I would never. And..." His voice gets so quiet, like he's scared to ask. "Will you stay for breakfast?"

Kieran cozies against him, grinning as he closes his eyes. "As long as you're cooking."

* * *

Of course, Seth turns out to be a real adult. The kind who gets up fuck-early in the morning.

Luckily, he doesn't try to rouse Kieran at whatever gross time it is. Even his slow and careful wriggling out of the bedcovers disturbs Kieran's slumber enough that Kieran groans at him, but Seth just presses a kiss to his forehead—Kieran grumbles sleepily—and slides out of the sheets, and then he's gone.

Kieran falls back asleep. He tries to, anyway. He wakes up after what feels like ten minutes when Dragon jumps up on the bed and walks directly across his tits.

"*Ow*," Kieran yelps. "Motherfu—" He opens his eyes to see Dragon circling back, evidently curious about his pain. She's purring, though. And she headbutts him even though he's glaring at her, and purrs all the louder when he reaches over to stroke her fuzzy head.

His clothes are folded politely on the bedside table. That is definitely Seth's doing, because Kieran is sure he abandoned them on the bathroom floor last night.

As he's struggling into his shirt and underwear, Kieran looks around, taking in the clean but homey state of Seth's bedroom. There's a framed photo of Dragon on the bedside table, along with an old couple who might be Seth's parents; there's a UC Berkeley diploma and historical maps of San Francisco and New York hanging on the walls. A glance inside Seth's dresser confirms that he absolutely does fold his socks and sort them by color. Dragon purrs like a garbage disposal and winds around Kieran's ankles while he grins involuntarily at the sock collection.

Then there's a desk, as painfully neat as the one he keeps at the office, but stacked with books and DVDs—Kieran catches sight of *Before Stonewall* and *The Celluloid Closet*. Further investigation reveals that the DVDs are mostly a collection of super schmoopy and decidedly unhistorical gay movies.

Honestly, he's never met a guy more in need of a boyfriend.

Kieran hopes he's up to the task.

He pokes his head outside the bedroom, and the first thing he notices is the smell of bacon and eggs floating out of the kitchen. Seth is humming to himself, and the pan is sizzling. Kieran scoops Dragon into his arms and goes to investigate.

"I think your cat likes me," he calls.

Seth peers out of the kitchen, a pair of nerdy reading glasses perched on his nose. Kieran grins at the sight of him. "Well," Seth says. "Good. I don't know what I'd do if she didn't."

"Kick me out on the spot, probably."

"Probably." A flicker of something—insecurity—passes across Seth's face. "Are you staying?"

Kieran smiles. "Yeah." He wanders into the kitchen as Dragon purrs into his shoulder. "Yeah, I think I am."

Breakfast comes served on fancy plates with a cup of coffee, black, no sugar. Seth has a cup of peppermint tea, and scrunches up his face when Kieran points out that he has a peppermint problem. Under the table, his foot rests against Kieran's ankle.

Kieran thinks about how every time he brings Seth a coffee, he's going to think of this. The smell of mint and diner food, Seth smiling, self-consciously pulling the collar of his pajama shirt up to hide the hickies on his neck. Kieran's never going to be able to look at his weird boyfriend across the office without grinning.

He could get used to that.

* * *

When the dishes are cleared away, Seth comes back to the table and clasps his hands around another mug of tea. Kieran can tell just by the look on his face that they're going to have a grown-up relationship conversation, and is surprised to find he's not actually dreading it.

Which is not to say that he doesn't open with sass. "Is this the part where you start asking me if I have any major allergies and whether I want two kids or three and what color I'd paint the kitchen?"

"Well," Seth starts. He looks a little embarrassed, but then he smiles. "I was going to lead with 'Do you want to watch a documentary sometime?' and 'Do you want this to be a relationship, or...?'"

"I wanna date you. Yeah." Kieran is not sure

he's ever been more certain on that point. And the look on Seth's face when he says it—tentative, uncertain, and so happy—is enough to convince him ten times over. "It depends on the documentary, though. Only if it's got a happy ending."

"Noted," Seth says. Then he tries to get serious again. "We should talk about boundaries. For the office, I mean."

"Sure. But can we make it fun?"

Seth raises his eyebrows. "Fun?"

"Yeah. Like while we're laying down the ground rules, we could be making out. And while you're brainstorming a list of all the things we can't say to each other at work, I could be sucking your dick." Kieran manages to get through the whole thing with a straight face, but doesn't last a second of watching Seth blush before he starts grinning. "Or we could just talk at the table. I'm cool with that."

Seth clears his throat and reaches across the table for Kieran's hand. "No," he says, to Kieran's surprise. "I think... I think your idea has some merit."

"Oh, does it?" Kieran's pulse kicks up a notch at the soft squeeze of Seth's fingers on his hand.

Seth's little smile reaches right into his eyes and warms Kieran down to his toes. "I can't take myself too seriously when you're around," he says. "That's a good thing. So—yes. Let's try it."

It sounds like he's saying yes to a whole lot more than kissing and ground rules.

Kieran swings out of his chair, pulling Seth by the hand, and drags him straight back to bed.

ABOUT THE AUTHOR

S. A. (Austin) Chant is a novelist, prize-winning pie baker, and ardent tabletop gaming enthusiast. They are the author of three novels: Peter Darling, Coffee Boy, and Caroline's Heart. They live in Seattle with a frightening amount of books and a cat who was recently described as a 'gooey cryptid'.

Find them at austinchant.com or at their Twitter, @essaychant.

CPSIA information can be obtained
at www.ICGtesting.com
Printed in the USA
BVHW042053151222
654320BV00011B/847

9 781087 878720